SESEN

EGYPTIAN LOTUS

Dr. Omnia El-Hakim

AuthorHouse™ LLC
1663 Liberty Drive
Bloomington, IN 47403
www.authorhouse.com
Phone: 1-800-839-8640

Published by AuthorHouse   05/28/2014

ISBN: 978-1-4918-6713-6 (sc)
ISBN: 978-1-4918-6712-9 (e)

Library of Congress Control Number: 2014903258

Acknowledgements

Omnia would like to thank her
children, husband and students for
their inspiration and support!

She is one girl; there is no one like her.
She is more beautiful than any other.
Look, she is like a star goddess arising
at the beginning of a happy new year;
brilliantly white, bright skinned;
with beautiful eyes for looking,
with sweet lips for speaking;
she has not one phrase too many.
With a long neck and white breast,
her hair of genuine lapis lazuli;
her arm more brilliant than gold;
her fingers like lotus flowers,
with heavy buttocks and girt waist.
Her thighs offer her beauty,
with a brisk step she treads on ground.
She has captured my heart in her embrace.
She makes all men turn their necks
to look at her.
One looks at her passing by,
this one, the unique one.

(Extract from a three-thousand-
year-old Egyptian papyrus)

Introduction

Mona Yusef is an anomaly in her native Egypt, a beautiful, ambitious, independent young Muslim woman whose dream is to be a successful engineer. Although her father supports her efforts in education, her restrictions of culture and religion continue to act as guides for Mona's decisions throughout her life. With the encouragement of her family, Mona travels the world to further her education which also leads her to a love that can never be with a Jewish student named Samy Cohen. Mona carefully chooses to abide by the cultures that appease her family and God assuming that the sorrow of her lost love with Samy will eventually go away. Through the trails of war, racism and oppression, Mona's education, career, marriage and children manage to prosper over time, and many geographies, as expected by her family and ambitions. Her past and her deep feelings for Samy are something Mona never expected to face again, not in the midst of her new life, let alone thousands of miles and memories from her native land of Cairo.

"Love has no other desire but to fulfill itself"
Kahlil Gibran

Contents

Happy Childhood

Egypt, the land of the pharaohs, was a quiet and calm country in the 1950s. The majority of the population was Muslim, but they coexisted peacefully with people of other faiths. The Copts, the country's largest religious minority, claimed descent from the ancient Egyptians. The word Copt was derived from the Arabic word qubt ("Egyptian"), and the Coptic language developed from ancient Egyptian. Tradition has it that Egypt was Christianized during the first century AD by the apostle Mark when the country was part of the Roman Empire. Thus, the Coptic Church claimed to preserve an unbroken line of patriarchal succession from Saint Mark. The Jews, another minority in the country, peacefully celebrated their festivals and followed their traditions amid Muslims and Coptic Christians. The flourishing economy had brought prosperity to many Jews in industry, banking, and commerce, and Jews occupied important social and governmental positions. During this period, the people of Egypt lived harmoniously.

I was born Mona Ishmael Ahmed Salah Yusef in 1947 to Ishmael and Fatma, a simple Egyptian couple, in Cairo, Egypt. We were a middle-class family with humble beginnings. Ishmael was a respected journalist for *Al-Akbar*, a popular newspaper, and Fatma was a traditional housewife who had been looking forward to taking care of her own family before the birth of her first daughter. Therefore, the day I was born, the couple felt that it was special, as though God had sent one of his prettiest angels to them. My parents, especially my father, pampered me, and much to their joy, the two daughters that soon followed. Our family lived happily in a predominantly Muslim neighborhood in the Moskey area, close to downtown Cairo, along with two Coptic Christian families and a Jewish family which also lived there.

Each day after school, we happily roamed free in the neighborhood. Playing with our friends and the other neighborhood kids was the norm, and always fun. All the while, our mothers kept a watchful eye on us from the balconies of the long, dusty street of high rise houses. Or at least high for us, and the world our little eyes saw. At this age, our eyes saw a world free from prejudice, fear, violence and life's challenges that were yet to come.

Beep, beep, beep, beep! I reach over and hit snooze. BEEP, BEEP, BEEP, BEEP! How did nine minutes pass already? And why is it so loud this time? I guess the day has begun and it is time for me to get out of bed. This time of year mornings in Montana are still quite cold from the low overnight temperatures and the thought of getting out of my bed wasn't motivating me to move very fast. I was also having such a surreal dream, which was so accurate to my actual neighborhood, our house and my mother's cooking that I hoped I may fall back asleep. I wondered if I had even been dreaming or if it was possible that I was just remembering in my sleep. Beep, beep, bee . . . I reach over and turn off the obnoxious alarm. Another nine minutes already? And with that thought I get up out of bed, slip into my robe and head for the shower.

2

Remembering

The air smells of spring and the weather has finally thawed enough to enjoy a hike. Although I usually ask my neighbor, Catarina from Spain, to join, I think this first walk I will inaugurate alone. Today I will head west along the creek. The sound of water and the crisp temperatures that linger along this edge, where melting snow has carved a steady flow through earth, might just be what I need. Rarely, but for some reason today, I need the solitude. Although I am accessible, even out here in the country, via modern technology, I don't take my phone along. It may be best to be alone from faces and extensions that keep my heart full and head occupied. Alone long enough to settle and remember.

After a slow pace, I pick it up and begin to move my arms. Maybe the physical distraction will keep the memories at bay a little longer. Then I flow back into a slower pace just as the creek flows beside me and alas . . . the memories begin to flood. I had not intended to think so much, but my plans to visit my deceased husband later must have begun the whole process and since he passed ten years ago, and I was married thirty-two, there was a lot to remember. Today is his birthday and after a long lapse, I will visit him.

I walked much longer than I planned, and found myself beginning to rush back home as, I still had a long drive to make to the cemetery. The invigorating and extended walk was refreshing. I made a cup of tea to help me linger in the tranquility that the hike had bestowed. A place that is much calmer, slower, quieter and more isolated than my routine life, is, and has mostly been. With my hot cup of tea and my clarity, I head upstairs for the master bathroom.

As I head down the driveway, I think about stopping for flowers to take to my husband's grave. Since he was more of a sweets person, it seems rather appropriate to take a pie, but I stop at the market for some flowers instead. I haven't visited in so long, I've sort of forgotten the protocol for this. It is not for any reason that I have chosen not to visit. As a matter of fact, I don't think I necessarily chose. Maybe the pain of the loss, I have not yet recovered or maybe the events since have kept me away. Regardless, today is the day and after a quick stop at the market, I can head for the highway which eventually leads to the cemetery.

I find a bouquet that I think suits the occasion as it resembles the tulip, which he had always bought for me since our move here to Montana. Not quite tulips, and unsure sure of their name, I'm content with the flowers as they looked a little like the lotus flower I was trying to match, that was so common back home. As I wait to make the purchase, I am approached by a young woman who asks me for a ride. I don't generally give rides, nor do I ever pick up hitchhikers, but this was a different situation as I was sure I had met this young lady before. I gladly asked her where she and the baby-to-be in her belly were going. She told me she needed to get to the shelter a few towns over and I, without hesitation, say, "I am heading that way." Through the tears she was unsuccessfully holding back, her soft and crackling voice responded with, "Thank you ma'am, I can't thank you enough." I touched her shoulder, offered a smile and asked her name.

Again a crackling, but stronger voice emerged saying, "My name is Jackie." "Have you eaten today Jackie?" I ask. And with a nod of her head I motion the direction of the car and add, "Well then, the car is this way."

While driving through the grocery store parking lot, and rows of cars, I tried to figure a way to ask what was going on with the young lady in the seat next to me. She couldn't possibly be more than nineteen, maybe twenty. A tiny, yet curvy little girl with long black, shiny hair. Her perfect complexion and dark skin tone were striking. And, although her black and slender face could hide any blemish it was completely free of any wrinkle or imperfection. Jackie was a young, beautiful black woman in a place that seemed far away from home.

It seemed that immediately as I merged on the highway, heading towards the cemetery, Jackie began to open up. "I haven't lived here that long, so I'm not real sure where I am going," she starts to say. "I think it's called, Haven House," as she states while also seeming to be asking me a question. "Well you are sure it's in Johnson, right?" I ask. "I am" she says as she laughs a little. And then as if remembering why she's going to Johnson, to the shelter, her face immediately returns somber and I can see she is frightened again.

Since we have a long drive together, I adjust the temperature in the car and turn the station to something I think the youth of today like to help distract the silence. Also, maybe, to keep me from asking too many questions. It doesn't seem to work as I utter, "So, how far along are you?" Then without pause, "Are you having a boy or a girl?" Jackie doesn't seem surprised or concerned with my line of questioning and responds readily, "I'm almost eight months." Then as if a little disappointed she adds, "I don't know the gender, Jimmy thought the surprise would be fun. But I guess that doesn't matter now." I already have an idea of what's going on, but I still ask, "Jimmy?"

"James Edward Wilson," she replies and adds, "I thought he loved me, but we can't be together." At this point I no longer have to ask, Jackie freely tells me her story of how she came to be in Montana, how she got pregnant and why she is alone. Her story is tragic, and started when she moved to Montana from the south, for college, and fell in love with a boy named Jimmy.

Her family's religious beliefs forbid her to be with a man of another faith, but Jackie stayed here to be with Jimmy when they found out she was pregnant rather than return home. The support of her family seemed unnecessary, at the time, as she was sure Jimmy loved her enough to take care of her and the baby. Otherwise, she told herself, why would he have walked away from a life of wealth and a secure future at his family's ranch for us?

Even the darkest of his parent's hatred and racism towards their relationship had, not yet, effected the love that she describes. At first, they devised a plan to be together and make it work, on their own. They agreed to have the baby. He agreed to get a good job, and she figured she could go back to school after the baby was born. "But then," Jackie slowly says, "We ran out of money and had no place to stay."

Apparently the job market wasn't what Jimmy expected and he ran back home to the comforts of his parents and money. The trade off, when returning home, meant leaving Jackie and never speaking of their interracial baby, which seemed easy for him to accept. Racism or not, their discrimination of her skin tone seemed to bother Jackie more than Jimmy actually abandoning her with nothing, and no way of taking care of herself or his baby.

Her father is a preacher at the church her grandfather started, so returning home was not an option. At least not one she was willing to try. I gathered that these events were recent and I hoped, for her sake, that she would try to call them soon. I didn't want to tell her how much she had ahead of her, and how hard it will be, so I instead gently say, "Family is unconditional and always come first, Jackie, and I'm sure they would welcome the call from you." Ready to change the subject, Jackie asks, "Where are you driving to today? I tell her to visit the cemetery in Larksville County. I further explain, "My husband passed away ten years ago and I'm going to visit his grave." At this point, the car becomes rather silent and stale.

Not sure if it was something I said, or just the fact that she's told her problems to a complete stranger and is stuck with me for a few more hours, all I can think to do is start talking. "I knew a girl growing up in Egypt, she was different, too. She was faced with a similar decision, but chose to do what her family, religion and culture expected." I continue to say, "Her story, although it happened long ago and far away, may remind you that the grass isn't always green on the other side."

Just as I pause for a moment to see if Jackie is interested in hearing the story, she excitedly begins rambling, "What's her name? Did she choose not to be with the love of her life? Was she pregnant?" Finally, to take a breath, Jackie stops talking for a minute and then proclaims, "Oh, do tell me what happen, we have a long drive ahead of us!" I settle in my seat, again adjusting the car's temperature and begin to narrate a story that was fresh in my thoughts. It was almost as if we put in an audio novel in the CD player as the words began to easily flow out of my mouth . . .

Little Mona was always different, even at a young age. Mona, who was usually in her pretty green twirled dress, looked like a ballet dancer. She wore cute, shiny black shoes with rounded toes like a doll and her zigzag silky socks looked like those of a princess. This particular day after school, Mona, dressed like a little princess was hunched over, her face a picture of total concentration as she watched her playmate make his first scooter. Her mother wrinkled her nose in disapproval. *Why doesn't she play with her dolls and the other girls?* She wondered. *What shall become of her?*

The Ishmael house was always bustling with friends and dinner guests, helping Mona to learn the importance of social events. Manners were extremely important in her family's culture, especially when they discussed politics. She learned the nuances of entertaining and the very polite ways people said no, including following a yes with another polite statement that meant no. For example, one may say no to more delicious food or dessert offered by the host in the first offering but accept it when repeated three times! Therefore, Mona never took as much food as she wanted to eat in the first helping when they were invited to dinner. Mona was sharp, so she stayed aware of what went on around her and made mental notes of things that might benefit her later on.

Most of the adult males in Mona's family, with the exception of her father and his older brother, were pharmacists. Her father's older brother was an actor in the theater, and the family didn't like that at all. Mona, however, looked up to him and was amazed by his natural flair for acting. He always entertained her and made her laugh when everyone else was so serious, as adults often are.

Fatma's father was from Turkey, and her mother was from Zakazik, a small delta town North of Cairo, but they now lived in the city. Mona's family and Egyptian friends considered Turkish people to be very wise, and Mona's Turkish relatives fit this generalization in her eyes. They also lived unusually long and healthy lives; Mona's mother's aunt had lived to be 100 years old, and Mona's mother's brother lived to be 105. Her Turkish relatives were always fun to be around, as they loved to tell stories to the kids and occasionally slip them a few *Maleem*, or coins equivalent to American cents, which seemed like a lot of money back then.

Outside of school, Mona joined the Egyptian equivalent to the Girl Scouts, and learned to swim, and play basketball and volleyball. Although a girls' club, Mona was more interested in the activities the boys were doing. She even went camping one summer, with the club, and learned so much that she couldn't wait to share with her friends in the neighborhood. In particular, she couldn't wait to share her findings with a boy named Samy.

Samy Cohen, a sturdy Jewish boy of seven with a mop of jet-black hair, didn't seem to care that his playmate was a girl from a different ethnic background; kids weren't bound by the unspoken norms and rules of society. Together, the children were building a scooter, a common toy in Egypt, with wooden sticks and nails. Mona, who was also seven, was fascinated by the way one could build things and how quickly he built the toy that went so fast, and her playmate seemed to share the same fascination.

The game of soccer had captured her attention, but she was strictly forbidden to play. This restriction had never made sense to her, and her numerous questions were always met with unsatisfactory, banal replies. She would spend time on the balcony watching the boys play, with a heavy heart. Cohen, what Samy went by, and most Jews in Egypt at the time, knew how much the game meant to her, and one day, he had gotten a ball made of discarded socks and asked her to play with him. That night, little Mona was the happiest she had been in a long time. Mona had always preferred riding bikes, playing with marbles, or even climbing palm trees when other girls her age were busy playing pretend with pretty dolls and kitchen sets in the corridors of their houses. Plus, the girls didn't want to play with her since Mona found it more fun to dismantle their dolls, and then try to put them back together.

On Tuesdays and Saturdays, Mona would watch a puppet show with Cohen and some of the other kids from the neighborhood. Ali, the entertainer, came by twice a week with his wife and his puppets, carrying a makeshift stage on his back to perform shows with songs and dialogue that mesmerized the children. Children awaited them eagerly every week, and their many surprises. With Cohen as her companion, Mona made sure she never missed a show, and she spent most of her allowance on them, too. She laughed and sang along with the performers, tossing her golden-brown hair in glee. Ali wondered about this little bright girl, wondering why she was always in the company of boys. *Ah, the unadulterated joys of childhood!* He must have thought.

Because Mona was the eldest child, she had an independent streak. She insisted on attending a coed elementary school called the Helmeya School until she was twelve. She then attended an all-girls' middle school and high school, as Egyptian girls and boys were customarily educated in separate institutions during the formative years from the ages of twelve to eighteen. Afterward, students were permitted to attend coed universities. Mona knew early on that she just loved school. She was the brightest in her class right from the beginning. She showed a natural aptitude for math, rather than the typical duties that young women generally began to master at this age. And her mother, Fatma, was paying attention with fretful concern.

Mona's mother was open-minded to a certain extent; however, she would have loved to keep Mona away from Cohen and the other boys and to engross her in chores at home. Being the spritely tomboy that she was, though, Mona always finished her housework in a jiffy and ran out the door in no time to go find the boys. The world outside presented opportunities for her to discover something new and exciting every day, which was reason enough for Mona to avoid staying at home. This was fine by Ishmael, as he didn't seem to say no to his headstrong and ambitious daughter much. Her younger sisters, on the other hand, met her mother's approval as a homebody who liked to help with household tasks. And luckily for Mona, this kept her mother off her back long enough for her to slip out to the next new adventure.

Cohen was born in Moskey and stood out among the other boys because of his peculiarly shaped nose. Honestly, you may have never known he was Jewish, or different than us, had it not been for his fair skin and very large nose. Mona knew that for Cohen, it wasn't fun being singled out and made fun of by the other boys. And although Cohen was the only Jew in our building, he always seemed to take the taunting well.

He enjoyed Mona's company, as she boosted his ego each time he tried something new. His mother wasn't too happy that her son had a Muslim girl for a best friend in Mona. And even though they were always together, she secretly hoped that it was a phase which he would soon outgrow. Cohen's father didn't have much of a say in the matter, or at least he never mentioned it, as this friendship grew and continued on for years.

Coco the Rabbit

Mona's love for cats and rabbits, among other animals, was notable. She once happened upon a rabbit scurrying around the neighborhood and immediately developed a liking for him. Cohen caught the rabbit for Mona, one afternoon, after chasing the critter around the proximity, and she was thrilled to have it. She declared him her pet and named him Coco, after Cohen of course, and he became popular with the kids and their parents.

Rabbit was a local delicacy and an ingredient in Molokhia, a green soup made with herbs and eaten with white rice, so Mona made it clear to everyone around that Coco was not for eating!

Despite of all this rabbit's publicity, however, he inevitably landed in a stew pot. Cohen's mother was of the opinion that Coco was better off as a meal at their table than if he was hit by a vehicle and of no use to anybody. Moreover, who could resist a free delicious meal? Cohen happened to have Mona over on the same day that his mother was cooking Coco, her much loved rabbit. Also invited for the feast of Coco, was a Jewish girl named Aria, who seemed to be Cohen's mother's beloved pet.

Mona asked Cohen's mother, "What's cooking? It smells really good."

"Oh, it's Molokhia!" Cohen's mother said as if it were no big deal. "Would you like to stay for dinner, Mona?"

At that moment, Mona knew for certain Coco was dinner, and she was shocked and horribly heartbroken. She took off in tears, stumbling down the stairs out of the third floor apartment that smelled of simmering stew. She felt suffocated by the very thought of Cohen's mother mercilessly killing her rabbit. She actually felt Coco's pain. She had kept Coco hidden, far from risk. Mona wondered if Cohen's mother could be so mean to kill him just to spite her. And did she invite Mona just because she knew how much she loved him, and how much his death would hurt her?

Realizing how hurt Mona was, Cohen ran after her to console her, but it was no use. Since he defended the murder, and murderer; he was weak in Mona's eyes.

Secretly, Mona had fantasized that the strict cultural boundaries may disappear and her and Cohen would find a way to be together . . . and live happily ever after. Much like all little girls, one can dream. However, it soon became apparent that this could never happen. Even if Mona got over and forgave the Coco incident, she felt Cohen's mother would always look for ways to assure that Mona suffered if she was with her son.

In these days, the Egyptian culture enforced the law that people could only marry those of the same religion. Families commonly arranged marriages at that time. Cohen's mother was a very mean and stubborn woman. Although she wasn't a very large person, her presence made her seem heavy and her demeanor was strong. She put on such a show of pampering Aria in front of Mona and saying that she would eventually be her son's bride. This deeply hurt Mona, because of her fondness to Cohen and her secret desires. However, she was also stubborn and kept it to herself by showing no sign of sorrow. Cohen's mother always got her way, and nobody, neither

her husband nor her other family members could convince her otherwise.

When Mona returned home, she wept uncontrollably, and her mother, Fatma, tried to console her. It was a while before Mona stopped crying, and by then, she had made up her mind that Cohen's family was evil and that they were incapable of thinking beyond themselves. The incident with the rabbit was deeply engraved in Mona's heart, and mind, and would remain with her for the rest of her life.

Mona's feelings towards Cohen's mother didn't improve any as Mona would run into her in social circles, and gatherings, over the years and observe her odd behavior. Egyptians socialized often, providing hospitality by serving food and beverages to bring people together, whether it was planned or not. Cohen's mother, who was of the Jewish culture, visited the ladies in the neighborhood but always brought her own snacks and tea and avoided eating any of those offered by her hostess house. Everyone in the neighborhood assumed at first that she didn't like them or their food, but over time they realized that it was, instead, so she wouldn't be expected to reciprocate the generosity to the ladies who visited her. This behavior was unacceptable to the cultural ways of the Muslim ladies. They still accepted her and invited her to the parties anyway, because as many before them had tried and failed; they were unable to change her ways.

In Cohen's family, too, his mother ruled the house. This was peculiar for Mona as the Muslim families she knew, including her own, were ruled by the father. Although, Mona really liked Cohen and the fantasy of a future with him, Mona didn't like the idea of having a dictator for a mother-in-law, and in her marital affairs. And this overbearing dominance of Cohen's cruel mother only further fuelled Mona's dislike for her. Mona's environment and the experiences in her life, as a child, were shaping her and influencing the person she turned out to be. Unfortunately, it seemed Mona's prejudice toward Jews began to surface at this early age.

Career Choice

Rural and lower-class Egyptians often believed that women were inferior to men. Women were expected to defer to senior male relatives, to avoid contact with men who were not kin, and to veil themselves in public. Girls learned to accept dependency on their fathers and older brothers, and after marriage, women expected their husbands to make all decisions. Historically, married life could be a time of extreme subordination and insecurity. The new wife usually lived with or near her husband's family and was expected to help her mother-in-law with household chores. The wife also faced considerable pressure from her husband and his family until she bore a son. Barrenness was a woman's worst misfortune, and not giving birth to a son was almost as bad. Women who had only daughters were derogatorily called "mothers of brides." Most couples continued having children until they had at least two sons. As the length of a woman's marriage increased and her sons matured, her position in the family grew more secure. A woman was at the peak of her power when her sons were married because she could then exercise influence over her sons' wives and children.

These patriarchal families valued honor (ird), the most important determiner of which was the sexual behavior of the women. Honor was essential to social life; without it, a family had no standing in the community. Men were especially concerned about honor. Women had to stay on their best behavior around men from other families to maintain their good reputation, as a bad reputation could disgrace a woman's whole family. A disgraced husband could restore his status through divorce, although most disgraced fathers and brothers believed that honor could only be restored by killing the daughter or sister suspected of sexual misconduct, and those who murdered these women were prepared to accept the legal penalties for their actions. These penalties were less severe in these cases than other cases of murders as such killing had some social acceptance. Mona was raised in a family that was against the murdering in the first place.

Over time, the progression for women's rights grew slowly. As it became socially acceptable for women to interact in their communities, many of them explored education outside of the home often in the same places as the men. Traditionally, women were preoccupied with household tasks and childrearing and rarely had opportunities for contact with men outside the family, but things had changed since the 1952 revolution, especially in education which now allowed many women to spend more time in public places among men who were not related to them. To limit women's contact with these men, practices such as veiling and gender segregation at schools, workplaces, and recreation facilities became commonplace. And in extreme cases, lower-class families, especially in Upper Egypt, tended to withdraw girls from school when they reached puberty to minimize their interaction with men. Mona's family never did believe in the old ways and kept her in school.

Mona was a very good student at school, particularly in mathematics and science, which was unusual for a girl in those days. Although academics were easy for her, her real love was the theater. The impression Ali and his traveling show left on her, since she watched the performances as a child, was inspiring. She also felt she had inherited the same talent for performing from her uncle and shared his love of the profession. Mona hoped she could become a professional actress. However, because women in her family didn't work outside the home, she had little hope of achieving her dream. She loved to act out roles and, in turn, people laughed. In high school, she performed in school plays, almost always in the lead role. If a play called for a male role, one of the girls in her all-female high school would dress up as a man. Mona never had any problems doing this because she loved to act, and it didn't matter which sex she played as long as she was onstage, and preferably in the lead role.

In high school, Mona also developed a passion for travel, which she inherited from her father, whose job as a journalist frequently took him to Europe and other parts of the Middle East as he gathered political news of interest for Cairo's readers.

At age sixteen, Mona graduated from high school with excellent grades. Cohen graduated at the same time with equally good scores. They had continued to be friends, but things had changed. It was now unacceptable for them to spend time alone, as Egyptian culture frowned upon interactions between unchaperoned teenagers. They met only at family events or on Fridays, when their families went on picnics to nearby parks. Mona found that the transition to the adulthood phase was difficult as she gradually lost her freedom which changed her relationship with Cohen. Mona could not play, joke or tease him as she used to do in their childhood. Her family closely scrutinized her every action to make sure that it was socially and culturally acceptable. For shaming the family name was not an option. She gradually became a quiet young girl, as expected by her culture, but she had a strong rebellious streak. She didn't like the fact that her mother didn't work or that men enjoyed advantages and opportunities that were denied to women.

She noticed that boys didn't get the same treatment, and she considered this unjust. However, she saw her education as a means of receiving respect and acknowledgment by the very society that chastised her as an inferior, and women in general.

Mona loved her Muslim religion because of its openness and honesty and its values of doing good and helping others. She had no problems with its principles, but she strongly rejected the chauvinism that resulted from men's interpretation and application of those principles. She resented that men considered themselves superior to women and that men expected women to follow their orders without question. In her eyes, she saw that her religion and culture appeared to consider women as objects limited to bearing and raising children and taking care of the household. Mona so hated this idea that she decided to do something different with her life.

After high school, Mona considered further education. In the sixties, the educational system in Egypt was very different from the system in America. The American system was open to all students. Students could apply to any colleges they wished and attend one that found their grades good enough. Once enrolled, they could choose whichever major interested them as long as they met the prerequisites and maintained good grades. Alternatively, students could attend community colleges to prepare themselves for admission to more prestigious institutions.

In Egypt, high school students with very good grades could go to the schools of their choice and choose any majors they wished, but students with lower grades had severely limited choices. For example, only students in the top 5 percent of their high school graduating classes were permitted to attend colleges of engineering or medicine. Therefore, many students were not able to enroll in their preferred colleges. Mona realized that educational opportunities were restricted for all students in Egypt, and particularly for women.

Fortunately, Mona's high school grades were excellent, so she had the freedom to choose among the top colleges in Egypt even as a female. Although her family allowed her to choose a college to attend, they had clear ideas about which major she should pursue. Mona hoped to attend a theater program to learn how to act professionally and direct plays, but her family objected. Surprisingly, even her uncle, the actor, was opposed because during this period, women actors were neither accepted by other actors nor respected by society. Even worst, often revered as undignified and loose, female actors at the time came with a horrid reputation. Worried about their reputation, Mona's family felt that her education should focus on acquiring skills and credentials that would prepare her for a more dignified career.

Ishmael, a proud father and accomplished journalist, had high hopes for his eldest daughter. She was not only beautiful but also had a sharp mind, so he was always worried about her and concerned for her next move. She was the *noor* ("light") of his eye, so he encouraged her to be the person she wanted to be, while also fearing what she might become. He envisioned her aiming for higher goals rather than settling down with a husband and giving up her talents and skills to live a mundane family life. A vision Ishmael had for Mona that Fatma, her mother, didn't always agree with.

Although Mona's choice of joining the theater was unacceptable, to placate her, Ishmael suggested that she get her basic academic degree and then enter the theater if she still chose to, in five years. He instead wanted Mona to put her exceptional math skills to use and become an engineer, although hardly any women pursued a career in this profession dominated by men. Fatma, on the other hand, couldn't support the idea of her eldest and most likely to wed first, not following in her footsteps of raising a family as a priority. Although there were many arguments in this regard, Mona finally agreed to first get her engineering degree and then work toward fulfilling her passion for theater. Mona's mother eventually also conformed to the compromise, only if Mona would agree to meet the many candidates for marriage that her mother had in mind for her.

Mona's decision to study engineering was easy because of her proficiency in mathematics and her like for construction. Although there were few female engineers in Egypt at the time, she liked the idea of pioneering the field. Plus, an engineering degree took only five years, compared to seven for a medical degree, which meant she could pursue her acting ambitions sooner.

Mona decided to major in civil engineering because of her fascination with bridges and her fond memories with Cohen. She started out wanting to learn how to design such beautiful structures as Cohen had done. Ultimately though, she became more fascinated with the structures in the city and her focus became on bridges, supporting heavy loads, and she thought she would never tire of looking for innovative ways to design and create heavy beams to transfer the populous, and often dangerous, traffic in Cairo. By the end of her degree, she had hoped to take part in constructing roads, bridges, and dams that would improve people's lives.

College

Mona enrolled at the Ein-Shams ("Eye of the Sun") University and became one of only four women in the civil engineering department that was also taught entirely by men. At the time, Mona was unaware that by simply sitting in an engineering classroom, these girls were challenging traditional views of what women could and could not do. It soon became apparent, to Mona and her female colleagues, that they were pioneers in a time of change.

The professors were clueless about dealing with the women in their classes, and the male students wondered what the women were doing in engineering classes and even found them to be a source of entertainment. They mocked the women's clothes and mannerisms and carried their equipment, as if they thought the women to be fragile. Some faculty members weren't keen on the idea of having females as their students, and those became evident to Mona immediately.

Mona and the other girls tried not to be discouraged by these attitudes and studied constantly, probably exerting twice as much effort as any of the boys in their classes, but earning half the credit for it. This experience showed Mona firsthand the disadvantages that minorities faced in school and in the workplace. And in this case, Mona being a young woman, was the minority. She, and her three female colleagues, worked twice as hard as their male companions but with the added pressure and fear that any slip somewhere might validate others' prejudice against them. Which would, in turn, further support the old ideas that they, or any women, did not belong in there.

Mona learned that being a woman in this environment wasn't going to be easy, and even under the worst of circumstances, she tried to remember her blessings. She was aware that even though Egypt was hardly an encouraging environment for women, her situation could have been far worse if she had been born in a more conservative country like Saudi Arabia. And although her upbringing was liberal, during the course of her years at college, Mona learned to face awkward moments of teasing, humiliation and ridicule by her male counterparts. Mona grew up fast, she was no longer naïve and understood that, again, her differences came with consequence. Fortunately, and by no coincidence, she was not alone.

Trying times bring people closer together, they say, and it was in the trying circumstances of college that Mona made two really good friends, Isis and Celia, both Coptic Christians. Mona and her friends were practically inseparable throughout their college years and got to know each other inside and out. They talked about everything from the latest fashions to school assignments, gossip, and even boys. They were each other's source of joy and encouragement, and they shared the same struggle against the inequalities they faced. Eventually, their male classmates' curiosity wore out when they realized that their female classmates meant business and were actually doing as well academically, sometimes much better than they were. They gradually earned the respect, and even friendship, of some of these male students. Some of the professors eventually got on board too, except for some that found it necessary to oppress the female gender.

One particular professor, Dr. Amir Shakir, had it out for all of the female students. It got to be pretty bad over the years with his comments and criticisms. And when the girls didn't respond well to his subtle, yet uncomfortable sexual innuendos, their grades suffered as a result. Furthermore, the girls felt unable to mention, report or protest his inappropriate behavior, or they would risk being expelled. Comments like, "Why are you in my class? Aren't you the secretary?", or "You're just like my wife, merely able to engineer dinner", became manageable for the girls as they learned to take it in stride. However, for Isis, Mona's best friend, school had become a place of fear, violence and danger, and Dr. Shakir was the cause.

The fact that Isis even mentioned the injustice was a miracle, as it brought her much shame. Dr. Shakir had forced Isis to engage in sexual acts that she eventually shared with Mona as she struggled with the fear that she was no longer pure, innocent, nor able to be married in a dignified manner. Without her consent, Isis had managed to shame her family name, disgrace her image in society and taint the laws of religion by simply pursuing her education. She endured this suffering alone, with just Mona knowing what had happened, and although she barely survived these events over the course of five long years, her consequence would have become a brutal and harsh reality if she had shared it with her parents, administrators or authorities. Isis, Mona's smart and beautiful Coptic friend, had to pay more for her education than the rest of the girls.

Being a pretty girl, Mona attracted a lot of male attention and admiration, and her friends kept her informed about her admirers, but Mona only had eyes for Cohen, who had also been attending the same school. Although he was studying electrical engineering and Mona's focus was on civil engineering, their paths crossed often. He always had a place in her heart, she knew Cohen felt the same, but Mona now knew a relationship was unacceptable in their society, not to mention in their families, for whom knowledge of their attraction would have been devastating. Over the years, Cohen's feelings for Mona became evident, in particular when others showed interest in her. Cohen was more open to a relationship than Mona and believed that they should let their families know of their feelings in order to come up with a solution. Mona didn't feel this was feasible, as she knew it would only cause trouble. So, Mona entertained the idea of other suitors, and there were many, and Cohen did not like it much.

Isis and Celia knew of the attraction, between Mona and Cohen, and had conflicting opinions about it. Isis thought Mona needed to think sensibly and follow her mind, as Isis had no interest in men and wanted nothing to do with them. But Celia, however, urged Mona to follow her heart as she had not been tainted like Isis, nor had she even know what happened to her. Mona did know about the travesty, and although it had not much impact on her decision with Cohen, she felt Isis supported her difficult choice. In the end, Mona decided that it was best that she follow her mind, not her heart, and tried to distance herself from Cohen, but as much as she tried to ignore him, it wasn't easy.

It pained her to see him in class, on campus and around the neighborhood in social circles. She couldn't put away her strong feelings for him, still. Wondering if she had made the right decision, she spent many nights tossing and turning trying to forget about him. Eventually, she learned that if she engrossed herself in her studies, projects, and work she had also found a way to survive. While at the same time excelling in school, she ultimately had no time to think of anything else. She pushed herself hard in her work, and studies, and made a point to tell herself every day that she could do this. And, that she could do it without Cohen.

Cohen was hurt at first, but when he tried to make sense of her behavior, he realized what she was thinking. He tried to speak to her alone on many occasions, but that wasn't easy since she was always surrounded by her friends. Mona knew that Cohen wanted to discuss the feelings they once shared for each other, but couldn't bear the conversation. Then one day after class, he happened to notice Isis and Celia leaving the college, without Mona, earlier than usual. He realized, and secretly hoped, that Mona was alone in the lab, and Cohen went to look for her so he could try, again, to talk to her. He quickly ran through the corridors looking through the windows of each room as if there were a fire drill occurring. He finally found her alone in the lab studying a sample of a brick. Out of breath, and without much thought, he blurted out, "I think I need to be a part of the decision since I'm involved in this too."

Mona looked up from her sample and stared at him in total confusion. "What are you talking about?"

"Don't act coy with me, Mona. I know what you're trying to do. Why are you giving up on us? We can make this work, you know. You can't cut me out of your life like this!" Cohen looked pained as if a tear was welting in the corner of his left eye.

"Listen, you know very well that our society will never accept us being together. We need to put our relationship behind us. We have no future. You're a Jew and I'm a Muslim. We can never be together," Mona said and started picking up her stuff to leave, as it wasn't acceptable for a young girl to be talking alone with a boy.

But Cohen wasn't convinced. "You don't have to leave; get back to your work. But I must tell you, religion and traditions shouldn't be obstacles to love; they should foster this noble feeling. Someday you'll understand, but I hope it's not too late then." As Cohen turned to leave the lab, Mona felt her heart sink deep into her core. Although she wanted to say something, anything, and maybe she even tried to mutter a word . . . she instead turned back to her workstation and picked up the brick.

6

Enter Omar

Omar was a handsome man, tall and well-built with a full head of black hair, hazel eyes, a small nose, and a rather defined mouth. Besides studying, he was involved with the school's soccer and basketball teams. He was very physically active and a star athlete to his teams. He came from a traditional Muslim family in a rather small rural village in Egypt, but by the way he carried and conducted himself you would never know. Always the class clown, and the life of the party, Omar was a rebel and pushed the limits of cultural and social norms. Mona could see though, that in his heart, he was a simple man who valued his family and relationships.

Omar was in his final year of college studying mechanical engineering, while Mona was a freshman. He had worked hard, so far, and focused on his studies to become somebody his family could look up to. Being one of the first in his long line of siblings to study at a campus, and successfully earn a degree, he had a lot at stake. He had never let any distractions bother him, not by anyone or anything. He respected women, but he kept his distance from them, and having only one woman in his department helped.

That all changed on the day he went to collect money due, from the students, for a summer research trip to Germany. As the president of the student union, he was responsible for organizing the trip. The moment he set his eyes on the girl wearing a colorful summer dress and high-heeled shoes, walking towards him, he became entranced. As she neared in her bright yellow dress, that flowed in the wind and seemed to accentuate her hips with each stride, he felt his breath speed with each increasing heartbeat.

As she approached Omar, she handed him her money for the trip. In a voice, that seemed to him to sound of an angel, she told him that the prospect of traveling alone for the first time was so exciting to her. Her big brown eyes peered at him with such enthusiasm and her face glowed like the sun, which also reflected shades of red in her long locks of hair, making her all the more breathtaking to him. He was at a loss for words, which didn't happen much, and didn't even look at the money that she handed over to him to assure it was all there. All he could do was stare at her with his mouth wide open. Omar was captivated by this girl and he just couldn't stop thinking about her after making her acquaintance that day on the campus grounds. Her name was Mona.

Mona was unaware that this behavior reflected his attraction towards her. All she saw was a supposedly responsible man staring at her, and that his mind seemed to be elsewhere. She had handed over her money and was waiting for her change, but Mr. Omar, as students called him, seemed to have no intention of returning it. *What an irresponsible and incompetent person he is!* She thought to herself. *Isn't he supposed to give me my change? Why is this guy our student body president? Mona, was not impressed.*

One of Omar's classmates eventually nudged him, and Omar realized what he was doing, or rather, not doing. He returned Mona's change and stared blankly at her as she left, laughing and chatting with her friends with complete irreverence towards him.

This was not the last of Omar that Mona was to see. For some reason, after their introduction, Mona and her friends seemed to see him all over. Each time, the moment he set his eyes on Mona, his face lit up with a goofy smile. Isis and Celia noticed this change and brought it to Mona's attention, but she just shrugged it off at first, thinking it to be a silly infatuation as she, now, revered him as an easily distracted man. He started chatting with the girls, and soon enough, Isis knew who he was, where he came from, what he and his family did, and everything else he wanted Mona to know about him. She and Celia knew that he was only trying to get close to Mona, but they liked their conversations with him as they were always in good humor. They would always let Mona know about his feelings, which she didn't take much stock in.

"Omar has this huge crush on you. Don't you see it?" Isis said. "He follows us everywhere like a puppy! How can you be so blind?" Mona could hardly believe this to be true because the few times Omar had actually spoken to her, he went dumb. Her response was always, "Oh, stop! I have no time for that!"

As time went by, Mona and Omar's chance meetings occurred more. In particular, they saw each other often to plan the trip to Germany and to work out the details of their stay. He sought her out, knowing her excitement for the trip, finding an excuse to be with her at every opportunity. This suited her well, as it helped her put Cohen out of her mind—not that she could ever forget him. Cohen was, after all, enrolled at the same school, but Mona did her best to avoid seeing him much. Omar seemed to be really looking forward to the trip, and she finally began to suspect that he had deeper feelings for her.

7

The Trip to Germany

The opportunity to travel abroad for the summer wasn't available to many students. Mona's family could afford the one-hundred-pound fee, so Mona considered herself fortunate and was grateful to her father for granting the opportunity. Of course, her mother was against the trip because in her opinion, Mona was too young to be traveling alone overseas. She thought Mona's father was crazy to allow it, but he said that he wanted her to learn, and to be independent, and that he trusted her because she was smart and had never made him worry. He allowed Mona some freedoms, but in many ways, Ishmael was also overprotective. His worries were those of all parents sending their kids off to school for the first time; he worried that she would drink alcohol, engage with boys or do something outrageous. However, he tried not to let his cultural background or his overprotective nature overcome his desire to encourage Mona's independence and to encourage her to take the opportunities available.

In addition to school, Mona was also fortunate enough to get a summer job in an engineering office in the heart of Cairo, while most of her fellow students worked as laborers in manufacturing plants in the industrial section. It just so happened that the firm needed a draftsperson in the drawing section where the engineers lay out the structure's dimensions and illustrate accurately the various cross sections of the design. Mona applied for the job and said, "I can do the work; just show me how." The System Engineer Manager, "the Boss", appreciated her confidence and charisma and hired her. Although she was still in school learning to do the job, she was a very fast learner and wasn't afraid of hard work or the challenge.

It behooved Mona that her boss liked her, and the work she did, in the short time that she was there as this made it easier to ask for the time off to go to Germany with her classmates, and Omar. You see, Mona's ambitions often overbooked her schedule as she stayed so busy all the time that she could hardly look, ahead, into next week. She was given the time off to take the research trip, her trip was paid for, her part-time job provided the spending money she needed and she had an admirer that would be there as well. The only thing she didn't know about was Cohen.

Mona knew that Cohen would have loved to make the trip to Germany, and although he was a good student, that alone didn't help in this matter. The expenses had to be met by the students themselves, and he requested that his parents lend him the money, and last Mona heard, he was waiting for their response. In the end, his mother being the thrifty woman that she was, made it clear to Cohen: "If you have such a strong desire to go on this trip, then get a job and make some money for yourself. You can't expect your family to pay for your entertainment." Cohen informed Mona that he wouldn't be going on the trip, as that wasn't a viable option for him, and time had run out for him to start saving.

Then, one fine summer morning, May 17 to be exact, Mona, Omar, and ten other students set out for Germany. Mona was only one of two women on the trip. They journeyed for ten days by ship, and because they didn't stop much along the way the students kept each other company. Mona loved to sing with the group, as it reminded her of her theatrics that were currently on hold. She felt free as she sailed the seas and Mona sang for most of the way, and Omar was always watching her but was somewhat reserved and never participated in the singing. He even seemed to be a little less of the life-of-the-party guy, a somewhat calmer version who still told the best Arabic jokes. His popularity and leadership put him in the center of every gathering, but he now seemed to carry a more mature demeanor, and Mona found herself starting to notice.

They arrived at their destination right as scheduled and departed the ship to find a new and exciting environment, and a very different terrain. Mona took a look around, inhaled the coastal air that was crisper than that of Cairo's, and settled her feet into the ground as she acclimated. Mona's fears dissolved into ease and she was eager for the change. Germany was a great place to be, especially during the summer. The students all stayed in Dusseldorf, a busy and thriving city, and soon joined their allocated workplaces where they would intern separately for the remainder of their stay. Here they would learn their distinctive profession, applying their theoretical knowledge in a practical environment and getting paid to do so by the hour. They learned valuable lessons like a good work ethic, living independently, managing their own expenses and they were also having a great time.

Mona had a blast. She was ecstatic. She learned a lot from the German people and their culture, including how to be prompt, positive, and efficient, to be conscientious about details, and to work neatly. The German people that she met were tidy, hardworking, and serious. Far different from the lively, loud and boisterous culture she was accustomed to. And, although, Mona loved to laugh, and the Germans she met were a bit more straitlaced, she still enjoyed interacting with them very much.

One of the more stern people Mona met was her landlady, Fraulein Olga. A tall, slender and rough woman who peered into your eyes as she spoke to you almost staring you down as if she must win each conversation. She gave Mona and her roommate, Zenab, a hard time if they laughed too loud, which seemed to happen all the time. Fraulein Olga was also very strict about cleanliness in her house and didn't like the young women leaving even a scrap of paper lying around. She definitely didn't approve of smoking cigarettes or staying out late, but Zenab always snuck out to smoke, and she always did it late at night.

Mona thought that under her rough exterior was a loving and caring person who much rather enjoyed having guests in her house than being alone. Fraulein Olga had no family, she lost her husband to war and they had a child, which everyone assumed had died since she never spoke of him; and the girls never dared to pry. Mona knew they livened up the old Chalet with their youthful, and often loud presence, and Fraulein Olga took care of the girls. Although at times Mona and Zenab resented the tight restrictions, they respected them (well, with exception to Zenab's smoking) and Fraulein Olga.

On the weekends, the Egyptian students went to each other's apartments to cook dinner, catch up and then they generally went sightseeing or to a movie. Mona mostly enjoyed walking outdoors touring the sites or renting a boat and exploring the waters with the new German friends the group had made at school. Omar gradually became more comfortable around Mona, and Mona often caught Omar looking at her with glazed eyes, then he'd blush and look away quickly, and then he'd repeat the pattern again. After a few rounds, he would then be embarrassed and fidget or leave the area that she was in, which amused Mona. Mona deduced that Omar, indeed, had a silly crush on her, however, to what extent she could never imagine.

Before the end of the four-month trip, Omar asked Mona and the other girls to visit Wuppertal, where he worked in a factory called Solingen that produced sets of silver spoons, forks and other utilities. Omar had been offered a job mid-way through his internship for his leadership and technical skills, and because of his concern with his future success, he naturally accepted. It was farther away from Dusseldorf than Mona had expected but they decided to accept his invitation and the girls headed for Wuppertal.

He received an employee discount of 50 percent from the factory, and he allowed the girls to buy anything they wanted with his pricing. Mona and her friends couldn't resist, and they had been making money all summer, so they each bought themselves a set of gorgeous silverware. Mona's set was the most expensive and engraved with tiny, fine carvings in solid silver that shined and sparkle in the light. It came with all kinds of utensils and since Mona didn't spend much time in the kitchen with her mother, she didn't know what to do with half of them. She also didn't know at the time that she would treasure that set, and that trip to see Omar, for years to come.

When the weekend was over, Mona noticed that Omar was constantly on her mind. Although this bothered her, she was more bothered that he hadn't been coming around pestering her, or following her, or even gazing at her! With the distance of his job, he didn't come around as much but Mona expected to see him when he did. Instead he seemed to get silly over another girl, the girl with the short blonde hair that Mona had only met when they visited Omar at the factory. Mona didn't know what she was feeling, and she didn't want to think about it. She decided that since the summer internship in Germany was almost over, she wanted to just enjoy the remainder of the time, and ignore Omar.

Then, a week before the return to Egypt, the companies the students each worked for invited them to a dinner banquet to bid them farewell and show appreciation for their good work. It was a gorgeous dinner at a very fancy hotel with large, bright chandeliers. Mona deliberately dressed in a tight, fine-silk topaz blue gown that was cut close to her body, showing off her curvy figure. She picked it up earlier in the week from a local boutique, along with matching teardrop earrings, as she knew she would see Omar.

Everyone enjoyed the food, music and dancing and Omar did finally come talk to Mona. She could feel his admiration towards her which made her delighted, and he even danced with her for the first time. Pleasantly surprised that he was a good dancer, Mona wondered why he had never wanted to before. Their bodies were close, and in synch around the room, she felt his tight grip around her waist and knew Omar wouldn't let her go. She trusted him. She had never been this close to Omar before, or any man. Mona felt slightly conflicted as she was enjoying herself; yet, she always imagined that it would be Cohen that she'd touch this closely.

When the party came to an end, Omar offered Mona a ride home, claiming the other cars had no room. This was Omar's golden opportunity. He knew it would be unlikely that he would ever be alone with her again, as once they returned to Egypt, Mona would be inseparable from, Isis and Celia, her two best friends. Omar began to fidget and seem antsy, and remained rather quiet on the ride. Mona wondered what was wrong with Omar, after all, they had been having such a nice time.

Mona noticed what seemed to be a frown on Omar's face and asked, "Is something wrong?"

Omar mustered all his courage and finally said, "I've been meaning to tell you something for a very long time. I know this may sound silly, but I haven't stopped thinking of you since the fateful day you handed me your payment for this trip.

I am madly in love with you, Mona." Omar was very nervous and he began to stutter while trying to say the words: "Will you marry me?"

After a long and slightly awkward pause Omar adds, "I don't expect you to answer me right away, but my feelings for you have only grown and I think you feel it too." Mona was utterly shocked but managed to respond to Omar, "How is this possible? We don't even know each other," Mona says, "I have to concentrate on my studies; I have no time for this."

Omar, seriously and quickly responds, "You don't have to be with me right away. You have three more years before you finish college, and I'll be around for most of it, even after I graduate. That will give you enough time to think about my feelings so you know that they're true." He takes a breath and pleads, "Please, Mona. Promise me you'll at least give this thought. Give me a chance to show you that I am the man of your dreams. Mona, I know that I love you and you can count on me now and forever."

The intensity of his feelings took Mona completely by surprise, and her mind reeled with so many reasons why this would never work out. Mona hadn't thought of marriage and instead concentrated on her studies. Egyptian girls were supposed to think about it so that when the opportunity came, they would take it. When she did fantasize, like young girls do, about marrying Cohen it only left her with pain. What would Cohen think? Why was she thinking about Cohen? With these thoughts running through her mind, one look at him was enough to make her say, albeit reluctantly, "I'll think about it, Omar."

Say Yes!

Mona and the group returned to Egypt after the summer, and life resumed as usual for all but Omar. Mona's pending reply to his proposal made him so restless that he could neither eat nor sleep peacefully, and this went on for days. Mona saw him everywhere now—in the halls, between classes and at break, in the library and on the way home. To add to matters, he now showered Mona with gifts as tokens of his affection at every opportunity. He had made it a point to collect pieces of jewelry and other souvenirs in Germany that Mona had shown an interest in. Mona found these gifts to be quite thoughtful, they surprised her and charmed her as well. Omar didn't ignore Isis and Celia, either, giving them little gifts as well, but he was careful not to embarrass Mona among her friends in the proper tradition of culture.

"This guy is seriously in love with you," Isis said one day. "Didn't we warn you about him before? What happened in Germany, anyway?"

Mona just smiled and changed the subject.

"What's wrong with him?" Celia continued in her usual blunt way, "Or, what's wrong with you?" Celia added, "He's definitely handsome, he's madly in love with you, and he belongs to a decent Muslim family. He even has good prospects as a mechanical engineer. What more do you want, Mona?"

"It's not that simple," Mona said. "You know my baba (papa); he would never approve a relationship while I'm still studying. Three years is a really long time for someone to wait for me. I just don't see it happening." Mona pauses, as if to see if she's convinced Celia yet, and then she continues on, "I can't divert my energy from my studies and career to this relationship. And a marriage would require me to care for my husband and have children and tend to all the household issues that come along with them. I'm definitely not ready for that yet."

"Who's asking you to settle down right away? You could just get engaged. You'll be able to get to know him better and have all the time you need to prepare for marriage," Celia rationally explains. Celia's insight had given Mona something to think about, but she wasn't prepared to decide—at least not yet. Isis remained neutral to the situation as she didn't trust any man, and in turn, never gave Mona any advice. Mona appreciated her friends, and talking with them, but the inevitable fact that she had never told them about Cohen skewed their perspectives about the matter. She couldn't help but wonder if they did know, would they, or Celia, give her a different direction?

Mona managed to involve herself in a few social activities on campus the next semester, but she spent most of her time studying. Then, six months after her trip to Germany, her mother told her that two young men had visited Ishmael to ask for her hand, but he had no interest in either of them for his first-born daughter. One of the two men was family related and the other one, coincidently, was a friend of Omar's.

To Mona's relief, Ishmael still thought she was too young to be thinking about marriage anyway, and wanted her to finish college first. He still considered her his little baby and wasn't prepared to see her married so soon. Mona had not told him about Omar's proposal because she didn't feel that it was the right time, especially if she actually wanted to entertain the idea. She especially feared that he would judge or pick apart Omar after seeing what he did to the other two fellows that came to propose. Mona hadn't tried to rush the process of developing into the woman that she was, she was changing though and the rest of the world saw it too. By now her father knew that something was going on, something was different with her and that Mona was growing up.

At the end of the school year, Omar graduated, but Mona continued to see him on campus. He remained involved in various college activities and athletics, and always attended the parties. Whether he was working, involved in a project, or attending meetings, he seemed to always be around. When Mona finished a class, he would be waiting near the door with a compliment or a small, but clever gift. Her girlfriends teased him. Her girlfriends teased her. But Mona still just wanted to study and not make a decision. School became more difficult, and with the challenges that still lay ahead for her, she couldn't fathom getting engaged as well. Mona didn't see much of Cohen on campus or socially, but she couldn't get him out of her thoughts as she factored Omar's proposal.

Egyptians are very conservative, and they followed an unspoken rule that young men and young women shouldn't spend much time together, unless the young woman had a ring on her finger. Dating and premarital sex were taboo, and young Egyptian ladies and gentlemen were all aware of it. Young people who weren't engaged but saw each other in public risked damaging their reputations and offending those who upheld religious and cultural traditions. So, it was protocol that young people would get engaged, spend time getting to know each other, and then get married about a year later.

Omar was a gentleman and was sensitive to Mona's needs, and he always came up with a solution to any doubts she had. He supported her studies, encouraged her dreams and career aspirations, and helped her with everything else. He respected her ambitiousness and wasn't threatened by it, as he believed that an educated woman was an asset to her family and added to her community. He also made it clear to Mona that their engagement wouldn't be a distraction, as he could help her with her projects.

After Omar graduated, he found himself a good engineering job that paid rather well for a desk position. After working at the company for a while and saving, he was then able to offer Mona a real engagement present. The gorgeous red velvet box consisted of a gold necklace, a ring, matching earrings and even the bracelet. Mona knew Omar did this so that they could see each other officially within the norms of their culture, and he let Mona know of his intention to do so even though she had not yet said yes.

"What will people think if I wear these?" Mona asked adamantly. "That we are engaged or a happy couple," Omar says with a smile. "That's not funny, Omar. I haven't said yes!" Mona exclaims. "Say yes, Mona. Say yes!" Omar again pleads while he's on his knees as he hands her a bright lavender Sesen. Mona, with the aromatic fragrance of the lotus flower presiding over them, finally says, "Yes!"

Omar's father grew up in a rural area, and his family preferred that he marry someone from the countryside, but his parents agreed to accept his choice to marry a woman from the city and expressed their willingness to meet her family. Now Mona had to face her family, and she was ready to do so.

Mona went to her mother first about Omar's proposal and also asked her to persuade Ishmael to accept the engagement. Fatma was shocked at the news, as she hadn't had a clue that her daughter had considered this marriage for so long.

When she recovered from the initial shock, Fatma said, "Two suitors already came for you, and your father was not at all pleased with them. How do you think I'm going to convince him to accept this man? Don't you know better than to go against what your father has in mind for you, Mona dear?"

Mona replied, "Omar comes to see me at college, and he's a nice person, but I'm not comfortable with him visiting me unless we're formally engaged. He's well educated, has a good job, and is sensitive as well as sincere. He understands that I'm ambitious and supports my dreams and goals. If we get along well, we can move forward with marriage, but if we don't, I'll return his ring. Do ask Baba to at least consider meeting him. Please?"

Fatma tried to subtly encourage the idea, but Ishmael adamantly refused to meet Omar, so Mona spent the next year getting to know him without a formal engagement. Her jewels remained hidden in a safe place, unless she was to see Omar and then she would wear some or all of them. Mona tried again to introduce Omar to her father, and again, Ishmael refused to meet this boy named Omar.

In Mona's final year of college, she had a heated discussion with Fatma regarding her feelings for Omar. Mona had rationalized her choice to marry Omar and found it easy to fall in love with him. It was hard for Mona to accept that she could never even try to harness a relationship with Cohen, but she had ultimately convinced herself that this was the case and that Omar was the better choice for her. Mona explained how much she loved this man, felt she had honored her parent's wishes and she was pleading for them to accept Omar. "You know your baba," Fatma said, "He hasn't changed his mind, and he'll make such a fuss. I don't see him accepting an engagement to Omar at this time either."

Mona continued badgering her mother and always cried to Fatma over Omar. Fatma didn't like to watch her daughter in pain over choosing between her family and the man she loved. Fatma, although rarely having to exercise the skill, knew how to get what she wanted from Ishmael, and so she demanded that he meet with Omar and consider the engagement to Mona.

The meeting didn't go too well. Omar arrived with his brother and father for the gigantic feast that Fatma had prepared for the occasion. Already you could see that since Omar came from a rural area, Ishmael felt his daughter shouldn't be expected to give up her urban lifestyle. Let alone behave like the women in Omar's family, as Omar's father expected that Mona give up her career and stay home to take care of her husband and the future kids. Since Omar came from twelve siblings, that scared Mona a little. Ishmael just didn't think that this guy, who came from a different social class than Mona, was an ideal match for his lovely, ambitious, and vivacious daughter. And he made sure everyone else knew it too.

Omar wouldn't take no for an answer, at least not so easily. He convinced Mona to persuade her father to meet him once again, alone this time. When she could finally arrange the meeting, Omar spoke to Ishmael at length and argued that he would always love Mona, stand by her, and support her in all her endeavors. He promised not to hinder her career goals, but rather support them. He also said that he and Mona would live in the city once they settled down together. But Mona's father maintained his stance yet another time.

Finally, after pressure from just about everybody in the family, over the course of eight months, Ishmael finally agreed to the engagement. Mona was relieved and happier than ever. Some fathers remain protective of their daughters all their lives and just never accept that their little girls have grown up and are going to leave them. Ishmael was one of those fathers, and his change of heart showed resistance.

Mona couldn't understand this behavior of her father. Was his desire to protect her, his first daughter? Was it instinctive, she wondered, or did her father worry about his daughter because he knew full well the intentions of young men courting nubile, innocent girls and their potential to take advantage of a young girl's blind faith? Was it that every father, having gone through courtship as a teenager, was aware of a man's intentions toward a girl? And Mona couldn't help but wonder what those "intentions" were. She tried to reason that all, or some, of these things probably made a father distrust any man of a certain age. Mona never got an answer to this question, and she never stopped thinking about it either, as it took years for her father to come around.

After a long delay, Mona and Omar were finally officially engaged in a small family ceremony. Mona was very happy, as an engagement was a special time in a young woman's life, especially in the Middle East. The prospective bride and groom had fun socializing, and Omar showered her with gifts. They planned to marry in the summer after her last year of college, and Omar was continuing to excel at his work.

As Mona worked through her last year of college, she constantly studied, and Omar ran errands for her so she could focus. Mona maintained that she intended to be ambitious, independent, and self-supporting and told Omar that she wouldn't be a traditional wife like his mother or sister were. She worried that he might not be comfortable with her role, and she also worried that they'd have difficulty meshing his rural culture with her urban culture, but she had committed to try. Mona wanted to do so many things in her life, and she hoped Omar could accept that from her once they wed. He assured her that he would, and Mona believed him, but her doubts lingered, as some things are easier said than done.

All the kinks in Omar and Mona's plans to start a life together were ironing out smoothly, however, Mona had one more matter weighing heavy on her mind: Cohen. Mona knew that she had to let Cohen know of her engagement to Omar before Cohen found out from someone else. She was at a loss for how to break the news to Cohen. Even though her engagement to Omar wasn't the real reason she and Cohen would never be together, she knew the significance of the news.

As much as she tried to believe that she had gotten over Cohen, deep within, she knew he would always have a place in her heart that could never be filled by anybody else. By this time, her family had moved away from Moskey to a suburb closer to the heart of Cairo, and Cohen's family had moved to an area out by the pyramids. The change of scenery made her separation from Cohen bearable, as she only saw him now occasionally, and rarely, at school.

The distance between them, however, didn't much affect the love they found for each other as childhood friends. Nonetheless, Mona knew that the deep, unspoken feelings she and Cohen had for each other were about to be sharply severed by her commitment to Omar; a man Cohen barely knew. Mona knew she couldn't hold on to Cohen forever, and it pained her that they could never be. Mona dreaded that the time had finally come to pick one man over the other, and she had chosen Omar, a good man who shared her faith.

Mona finally found her chance to speak to Cohen on campus one day. She saw him sitting alone in the cafeteria and summoned all her courage to walk up to him and break the news that would change both their lives forever.

"Hi Cohen, It's been a long time since we've met, hasn't it?" Mona said as she sat at his table. "How have things been?" She adds.

"Stop making small talk," Cohen snapped. "I know you have something to tell me, and from the look on your face, I assume it's not going to be good news."

"Actually, you're right. You must have heard about Omar and me by now. Things have moved faster than I expected them to, but I've made a decision and I thought I should tell you." Cohen doesn't look up at Mona as she continues to say,

"We're not children anymore, and our decisions have consequences we may have to bear all our lives. Our society isn't fair to the likes of us, Cohen. You and I can never be together without hurting and shaming our families. I see no future for us, so pursuing one would be pointless. I've given this matter a lot of thought, and I've decided to accept Omar's proposal." And if that wasn't enough to devastate Cohen, Mona adds, "We are to be married soon. I suggest you forget about me, Cohen, and move on with your life as well."

Cohen was hurt, but his self-respect and ego wouldn't let him show it. He maintained his composure and said, "If you've made up your mind, then I have nothing to say. I wish you a happy married life with Omar. I hope he is a good man for you Mona." With that, he got up and left Mona sitting at the table all alone. Unable to move or say anything, Mona felt the familiar sinking, of her heart, into the deep of her core begin to reappear as she watched him walked away.

Big Fat Egyptian Wedding

The bridal procession at an Egyptian wedding gave new meaning to the phrase "making an entrance." The bride and groom, dressed in traditional Western attire of a white dress and a black suit, traveled to the hotel or wedding hall together. If they proceeded directly from the marriage ceremony at a mosque, they traveled in a wedding car decorated with flowers and ribbons. Family and friends surrounded them in their own cars, honking continuously to let on-lookers know that a wedding had taken place. When the bride and groom arrived at the reception venue, a parade of dancers and singers known as a zaffa, met them. *Enthusiastic friends and family members as well as hired musicians and often belly dancers made up the zaffa which followed the couple into the party.*

Then, the bride and groom sat in raised and decorated throne-like chairs at the center of the room as though they reigned over the party like a king and queen. Guests toasted the couple with a special drink made of rose sherbet.

At an Egyptian wedding, the focus is on the food first, then the celebration comes after and guests stay much longer than traditional Western weddings. Parents and friends gave speeches, and the bride and groom occasionally gave speeches of their own. All the while, music played, dancers danced, and friends may have dragged the bride and groom out onto the floor separately to dance. Male friends of the groom sometimes even tossed him into the air.

Then dinner would be served. This was usually a great buffet of all kinds of Egyptian food, with several kinds of salad and meat dishes such as kofta, kebabs, grilled chicken and fish, and saffron-flavored rice. For dessert, in addition to a Western-style wedding cake, baklava and other layered honey-soaked pastries were served. In keeping with Muslim laws, no alcohol would be served.

In rural areas, after the zaffa, the wedding ceremony usually took place in a big clearing of land under a huge

Arabic tent called a sewan. *The entertainment included a belly dancer, or singer, or both. Drinks, food and refilled plates were served to guests. The customary food, in this rural region of Egypt, is Fattah; made of pieces of lamb meat embedded in rice and bread and slow-cooked in stew. The bride and groom would leave the wedding early, and the guests would continue the festivities into the morning hours.*

Whether rural or urban, weddings reflected the unity of the families that have come together. Both families showed off their offspring and wealth to their guests. Thus, Egyptian weddings weren't just an announcement of marriage but also an announcement of the economic positions of the families, and a time to celebrate much earned bragging rights.

Mona finished her bachelor's degree with honors as planned. Although her father seemed happiest about this, Omar was happy too, as it signaled that their marriage was finally approaching. Mona's family held a graduation celebration at their house full of relatives and friends, decorations, and lots of food and hibiscus punch. A belly dancer performed as the spotlight of the party, which was as successful as a wedding celebration because the guests had just as much fun.

Ishmael was proud that his eldest daughter was now a respectable and well-educated female engineer, the first in the family as well as the surrounding community. Cohen graduated at the same time, but to Mona, he had to no longer exist in her thoughts.

Soon the fanfare died down. Mona got a respectable job at the Ministry of Water Resources in Cairo. It wasn't easy for the ministry to hire her, though—not only was she a female who wore high heels and dressed well, but she was also stunning. At first this was too much for them to handle, but the hiring manager eventually overcame his prejudices and gave her an opportunity. And also because he was sure she wouldn't succeed, thinking that she would give up once she was married and had children. Time proved him wrong. Mona totally engrossed herself in her work, mostly in an attempt to forget Cohen, their love and her past, but also to start her new chapter with Omar and their new life.

The time eventually came for her to fulfill her promise to Omar. Her father could no longer oppose their marriage now that she was engaged, had gotten her degree and found a job as well. Omar, too, was doing very well for himself. He had found a house to rent in a good location in the city, and he worked as a mechanical engineer in the army now, a prestigious job that paid three times the amount that non-army engineers earned.

So on a sunny, humid and beautiful day, Mona and Omar were married in Cairo in the summer heat amidst their friends and family and almost all their neighbors. Mona didn't care about the large crowd that arrived for her ceremony, she was happy to marry Omar and she loved all the attention. Omar was ecstatic to finally be united with the love of his life, and the sight of her in a white gown and long veil took his breath away. After the couple took their vows to spend the rest of their lives together, the banquet and celebrations lasted late into the night. Mona wondered what Cohen was doing that evening, but the thought didn't last too long.

The next day, Mona and Omar left for Alexandria on their honeymoon. They had a wonderful month at a beachfront villa with all the amenities. They learned about each other, explored the intimacies of marriage and had the time to consummate their exciting new love. The beaches, restaurants, and each other's company made it a romantic and memorable time for the young couple. After the honeymoon was over, Mona slipped into family life and effortlessly managed both her home and career. Omar was content with his job in the army, and Mona was happy with her decision to marry Omar.

10

The Six-Day War

At the beginning of the twentieth century, the Jewish community exercised remarkable influence in industry, commerce, culture, and the professions in Egypt. The Arab revolt in Eretz, Israel from 1936 to 1939 marked the beginning of the deterioration in the Jews' situation in Egypt, as they faced continuous harassment. During demonstrations against the Jews in 1945, protestors looted Jewish-owned shops and synagogues, and after the UN partition of Eretz, Israel in November 1947, Egyptian authorities held Jews hostage, confiscated their property, and arrested many. About half of Egypt's Jews immigrated to Eretz, Israel, so by 1956, only about forty thousand of them remained, and following the Sinai Campaign of 1956, many more fled to Israel.

The 1950s saw the rise of Gamal Abdel Nasser as the leader of the Free Officers, who overthrew the reigning king, Farouk. Nasser had revolutionary ideas that not everyone agreed with, but the promise of freedom and independence he offered were irresistible to the Egyptian people, as Nasser inspired the people to govern themselves independent of influence from America, Russia, or any other country. He became a popular leader, and the people were happy, at least in the beginning. Nasser was also a leader in the non-aligned world and an Arab nationalist, but his attempts to bring Arab countries such as Syria, Lebanon, Jordan, and Egypt together were not very successful. Although he tried to keep his country free of influence from superpowers, he became heavily involved with the Russians, accepting Russian support for the Aswan High Dam project, and many Egyptians objected to that. He was repressive, governing like a rogue dictator and putting wealthy people and his political opponents in jail. Still, he remained popular with the people because Egypt was finally independent.

By the early 1960s, he coerced the remaining Jewish people in the country to leave to Israel, and by 1967, only about 2,500 Jews remained in Egypt. When the Six-Day War broke out, all Jewish men were arrested. Nasser continually stated his intention to attack Israel and declared that other Arab nations should support him.

Israel had its own reasons to take over the Palestinian disputed land: they believed it to be rightfully theirs and under the leadership of then Minister of Defense Moshe Dayan, the country responded preemptively to an imminent attack and began what became known as the Six-Day War of 1967.

In 1967, Mona heard word that Cohen had left Egypt with his family and gone to Tel Aviv, Israel. She was relieved to know that he was safe. She was also glad that she wouldn't run into him anymore. Now she could save herself the pain and suffering that her inability to express, or admit, her feelings had caused. Now he was gone forever.

Mona now worked in a research laboratory conducting soil analysis as part of the construction of the Aswan Dam. She became intimately aware of the Russian presence in her country, which she noticed as tensions rose at the lab and at professional meetings regarding the Dam's construction.

Soon after, they learned that Omar had to prepare to leave with the Egyptian army for the war against Israel. The television and newspapers were full of stories about Israel's army also drafting their able men, and the inevitable war to come. Mona prayed for peace, and she secretly worried about Cohen, too. It wasn't long before she heard, from Celia who now worked for the government, that Cohen had also been drafted. She was torn apart, as both of the men she loved would be fighting against each other. She also knew that neither of them, would ever imagine, nor have any intent of killing the other had it not been for the war. Life to Mona now seemed so futile if decent, peace-loving people could be forced to fight by leaders determined on fulfilling their selfish personal agendas by making war.

Mona learned she was expecting her first child amid the tension in Egypt. And because Celia's job allowed her access to records, she knew things before anybody else did. Mona again, heard through Celia rumors that Cohen had gone missing on the battlefield and that he could be dead. She refused to believe the stories but was nevertheless shaken by them. She continued to pray for peace and the safety of the men at war. In particular, the two men closest to her heart, and on opposing sides.

During the fourth day of the war, on the frontline, Omar rode in a jeep with other troops, he stopped the vehicle as he spotted a small rock reflecting in the desert sand. As he focused on the rock, that wasn't more than the size of a coin, he saw that it was miraculously marked with an impression of the Virgin Mary carrying baby Jesus in her arms.

He got out to pick it up, and at that moment, the jeep and his colleagues, were blown away before his very eyes. He was the sole survivor of the blast. Alone in the middle of nowhere, on the frontlines of war, Omar walked all the way from Sinai back to Cairo. A trek that took him a far distance through unfamiliar and unsafe terrain some 442 kilometers, or 275 miles.

Omar reached home, dehydrated but alive and grateful, just as Mona began to experience her first contraction. Mona felt, at that moment, as though God had sent him home just for her. Omar was very thin, bruised up with wounds and he looked, to Mona, as if he had rapidly aged. He was heavy, it seemed to her, in both his head and heart and she was concerned with Omar's well-being upon his return. He immediately drove her to the hospital, where Mona delivered a beautiful girl and named her Yasmeen after the flower. Omar, although happy for the birth of a healthy baby, was still torn by the traditions of the culture. And as such, a bit disappointed that his first born was not a boy. What Omar had seen, faced and done in the war had hardened him and Mona could tell that her husband was torn internally, and emotionally. As he headed to meet his new baby for the first time, Omar brought two lavender sesens, one for Yasmeen and one for his love, Mona.

Soon afterward, Omar felt obligated to his battalion and returned to war, the way he had come, to his base in Sinai. He kept the rock with him throughout the hardships of the war, as that sacred rock was the reason he was still alive.

11

Peaceful Coexistence?

The Six-Day War indeed lasted for six days, and then the surviving men went home. There were a lot of lives lost, particularly for Egypt. Egypt had lost, but life returned to normal. President Nasser declared that he intended to assume full responsibility and resign. Many Egyptians didn't understand how he was still governing the country, but it seemed that in third-world countries, elected leaders stayed on until they died, as though they thought their countries wouldn't survive without them in power. Many people were upset by the possibility that Nasser would leave power and demonstrated in his favor, crying, "We want Nasser!" Thus, he remained in power, but not for long, as he died a few years later.

Anwar Al-Sadat came to power immediately thereafter, in 1970. President Sadat's leadership style was very different from Nasser's. In his eleven years as president, he departed from some of the economic and political principles of Nasserism and reinstituting the multiparty system. He broke ties with the Russians and pursued friendly relations with the West. His government was more transparent; He was more open to diplomacy and friendly foreign relations. Anwar Al-Sadat worked to repair Egypt's ties with the United States, and he showed a willingness to consider making peace with Israel.

Then, in October 1973, Egypt invaded the Sinai Peninsula through the Suez Canal and regained the territory Egypt had lost in 1967. Sadat contacted the United Nations and offered to negotiate a peace agreement with Israel. He offered a peace treaty in exchange for the return of the Sinai lands and went to Israel to meet with the Knesset and other political leaders. For this visit to Israel, and the Israel–Egypt Peace Treaty that resulted from it, Sadat was posthumously awarded the Peace Abbey Courage of Conscience award on September 11, 1991. At the time, however, this treaty was enormously unpopular with the rest of the Arab world and with Islamists, and Egypt was eventually expelled from the Arab League. President Sadat served Egypt from

October 15, 1970, until his assassination on October 6, 1981.

Omar returned home from the war safely, and as far as Mona had heard, Cohen was back in Tel-Aviv. Omar continued his job in the army, and Mona returned to full-time work determined to prove that she could be both a mother and an engineer. Mona had given birth to another child by now, Anwar, her second-born and their first son. They were elated and Mona was busy managing both children, Omar, her household and her career.

This was often an overwhelming challenge, but Mona was so full of enthusiasm that she was determined to do it all. Eventually, she hired a nanny to help with the baby and a maid to help with the cooking, and Mona also received some help from her mother, who lived close by. It was customary for upper-class families to hire maids and nannies to live with the families and help raise the children, while often being raised themselves as they might have come from poor families or been orphans. For Mona, it was the perfect solution to her busy life as she found balance with the live-in help and was able to spend more time with her husband, Omar.

The time Mona and Omar spent together brought them closer, although it also showed them the side of their partner that they hadn't yet discovered, and didn't always like. Although Omar was a loving and caring husband and father, he was always busy with the army, and he had one trait that really bothered Mona: he was extremely overprotective and subject to terrible jealousy. Since Mona was so focused in college, and not interested in suitors, she had never saw this trait in Omar until they were married.

Mona turned heads whenever she and Omar went out together. Omar grudgingly observed how men would stare at her whenever she walked into a restaurant, and he then became extremely jealous. If the butcher gave Mona a good piece of meat, Omar would accuse her of flirting, and they would fight. He also found it disagreeable that Mona accepted a lift to work, from a male coworker, when her car broke down and was in the shop.

Mona found his behavior illogical and silly. "Why shouldn't I ride with him, Omar?" she said. "You know him and his family, and we're adults. What's the problem?"

Another time, Mona asked one of his fellow soldiers for a ride, and when Omar found out, he was furious. This caused another big fight that ended with Mona and Omar spending the night in different rooms.

Mona appreciated Omar's good qualities, so she tried to put his jealousy in perspective, but he felt this way often, and Mona didn't know what she could do to assuage his insecurity. She wondered at times what might happen if he got an inkling of her dormant feelings for Cohen. She tried to remind herself that he was a good man who was concerned about his family, and that his overprotection was a sign of love, much like her father was. It did not make sense to Mona to change her behavior simply because of his attitude, and she refused to let his insecurity control her life. Therefore, she let him get upset every once in a while and hoped that he would outgrow these silly tendencies. The two children, Anwar and Yasmeen, were growing and the family seemed to be getting along and, overall, adjusting just fine.

A few years later, Mona was given the opportunity to travel to Italy for eight months to study and work on a project there. She thought it would be good for her professional development, and Omar supported her decision to go, so she left the kids with their nannies and invited her aunt to stay for the duration. Mona had traveled since Germany, but this was the first time she would be away from her children for so long.

Mona left Egypt, and over the next eight months, she learned many lessons in Italy. Her research was successful, but she constantly missed her children and Omar. She determined that if she were offered any more opportunities to travel, she wouldn't accept them unless she could take her whole family with her. Mona was counting the days in Italy until she could see her family, while also trying to enjoying the beauty and charm of the land.

One summer afternoon, towards the end of Mona's stay in Italy, the crackling intercom above her desk turns on abruptly with the sound of static fuzz and then the silence before a woman's voice starts speaking and pages, "Mona Yusef, telephone. Come to the office for a call . . . Mona Yusef."

Upon her arrival to the office, Mona grabs the phone cord and places the receiver against her ear, her mind wonders who it may be. Enthusiastically, she says, "Hello, this is Mona." There's a silence on the other end, yet she knows it is Omar. "Omar, is everything okay?" Still, there is just silence and she begins to feel unease as he never had called her at work. "Omar! Are you okay? What happened?" she says with an escalated and frightful tone. "Mona, oh Mona," Omar barely utters. Then through his tears, and a soft tone that she had not known Omar to possess, he adds, "Anwar is dead." The familiar feeling of her heart sinking into her core began.

She felt a flood of heat releasing in her body. Although she wanted to scream and release her pain, she wondered why she couldn't even cry. Mona was rarely silent, but now she couldn't speak and she couldn't go back to work. She could barely believe what she had heard. Mona left for Cairo the next day to bury her first-born son. The loss was much to bear for her and Omar, but Mona tried to continue on for Yasmeen, and the desire she once had to have more children.

Time past, and they found a way to cope with the loss of Anwar. And as such, the years that followed were generally happy ones. Omar found success in his military career, and Mona also found success in her work. They had a wonderful family, although small, and a comfortable life.

Mona became involved with the Egyptian Engineering Syndicate Union, where she focused on increasing diversity, particularly among women, in her field. She often participated in the Syndicate's discussions and offered her perspective, trials and experiences to an audience of men. She was the only female in the syndicate then, but the other members knew her husband and knew that she had her family's support, so they encouraged her to talk openly about gender equality and issues women faced in engineering. Mona's fellow members received her with respect.

She spoke persuasively while conscious that even the tone of her voice might influence the opinions of the people sitting around the table.

Mona was a great admirer of President Sadat, and she believed that he was a brilliant man and one of the best leaders Egypt had ever known. He opened the economy for private business and industry, as he was a liberal thinker and pursued an American-style approach, but many people, especially religious extremists, didn't like that. His wife, Jihan, was a pioneer for women's rights in Egypt and was instrumental in passing the Egyptian Civil Rights Law, which gave women more freedom. She was integral in improving Egypt's education system and started other programs that benefitted the youth, male and female alike. The extremists didn't like that either.

The country's progression was most encouraging for Mona to keep achieving in her career. Again, Omar had been drafted for Egypt's war on Israel to re-claim control of the Sinai region, with an undetermined return date. Upon his departure, Mona wanted Omar to know she was pregnant with another child. Although too soon to announce the pregnancy to their families, she felt it important to tell him before he left. As now, Mona knew that returning from war was never guaranteed.

In due time, Mona gave birth to another child, Asma. She was a beautiful little girl, with a full head of black hair, little ears and fair skin like her mother. Omar was at war at the time of Asma's birth, but rejoiced in the news that he received while on the front lines. Omar was now a Brigadier General in the Egyptian Army, and led his battalion into the depths of the war. Mona rejoiced that Omar was still alive and that he somehow managed to send a bouquet of flowers for the birth . . . twelve lavender Sesens.

Opportunity Strikes

Mona was effortlessly adjusting to her life now with a good job, two beautiful girls, and a caring husband. She was grateful that she couldn't see Cohen, but Celia, who was still Mona's best friend, kept in contact with him. Mona would catch herself asking Celia about him, feigning nonchalance about her curiosity.

In 1976, Mona met Dr. Johnson, a professor of civil engineering at Montana Tech who was living in Egypt and involved in a collaboration with the Ministry of Water Resources. The project was designed to help Egypt find ways to irrigate its crops, and hopefully, improve agricultural yields to the benefit of the country. The program also gave Egyptian engineers and scientists the opportunity for additional education in the United States, which would, in turn, further benefit Egyptian agriculture and industry. Mona's job required her to help Americans in Egypt understand Egyptian culture and facilitate their adjustment to their new living conditions.

Like most Egyptians, Mona had a favorable opinion of Americans and welcomed the increased contact with them. Egyptians also saw that their involvement with efforts in the United States benefitted their county, and saw it as a way to further support Egypt's efforts to shift reliance from Russia to the West. The transition was well on its way, partially because of President Sadat's vision and leadership. Most people also saw positive results from the private ownership of business and felt that this, too, was right for the country. Opportunity was abound for all.

One day, Mona's superior, Dr. Gamal, summoned her to his office for a discussion, and when she arrived, she was surprised to find Dr. Johnson there as well.

After the normal pleasantries, Dr. Gamal said, "Mona, Dr. Johnson has a really good proposition for you. He believes that you're a good candidate for a Ph.D. He thinks he can get you admitted into a good program in the States, which will increase your professional status. What do you have to say about that?"

Mona was put on the spot to respond, and because her experience of living alone in Italy was still fresh in her mind, she replied, "I think it's a great opportunity, thank you. However, I'm afraid I must pass, as I have my family to think about, and I'm content with my work here."

Dr. Gamal shook his head in disbelief and said, "Do you even understand what an opportunity this is for you? You're focusing on only one aspect of the situation, Mona. Please take a day to go home and think about it and speak to your husband, and then you can make a well-informed decision." Reluctantly, Mona agreed to consider.

When Mona returned home, she told Omar casually, "You know what happened at work today? They offered me the opportunity to pursue a doctorate at a university in the United States. You'll be happy to know that I turned it down."

She was sure that he would agree with her decision, because he was in the army and couldn't leave the country so easily, but to her surprise Omar said, "Are you crazy? Why not take it? That's a really good opportunity!"

A little surprised that she had to convince Omar, Mona explains, "What about our kids, your job, our house, and our families?" After a quick pause Mona added, "Such a change won't be so easy, you know! I chose to travel to Italy, and, Omar, you know what happened then. I'm not going anywhere without you and the girls!"

"Let's not make a hasty decision, Mona. Your Baba and Mama are coming over for dinner, so let's ask their opinion before you refuse the offer. Such an opportunity may never come by again, so let's think it over," Omar pleaded.

Mona grudgingly agreed. That evening over dinner, Omar brought the topic up to Mona's parents. Ishmael was happy, and proud, that his daughter was fortunate enough to get the opportunity to study at a prestigious university in the United States, and he suggested that she accept the offer and that Omar and the girls could eventually follow her.

Omar said, "I only have a year left in my obligation to the army, so I can take care of the kids for that time. Besides, my aunt can come help take care of them as well." Much to Mona's surprise, Omar continued to say, "I was actually contemplating leaving the army and moving us to a more liberal country. The US will be an ideal place for you, considering how independent, smart and outspoken you are."

Ishmael added, "Your girls will be my responsibility while Omar is away for army duty. We can work the arrangements out, Mona. Then, once you're settled, you can take the girls, and they could get an American education too."

But Fatma, Mona's mother, wasn't convinced. She lashed out at the men while saying to Mona, "Men can only talk. There's nothing missing in your life! You have a good job and two beautiful daughters. If you really want to study, why don't you study here? We have good programs here, too, that you have helped provide through your work." Fatma pleads with one last attempt at Mona, "Children need their mother. Besides, I have a feeling that you won't come back to Egypt if you go to the states."

Mona thought deeply about the opportunities that were before her as she listened to everyone's opinions. If she went to America, she would not only receive the best education, but she would also enjoy the independence and freedom the American culture offered. Glimpses of images she had seen on television floated in her head, especially of Elvis Presley, who was her all-time favorite. Deep within, she also thought that by leaving Egypt, she would put more distance between her and the memories of Cohen. Her trip to the United States, maybe then, would break the last link connecting them.

Finally, she announced to her family that she had decided to speak to Dr. Johnson and accept the offer on the condition that she could take her daughters with her. The nanny then offered to accompany her to help with the house and kids so Mona could focus on her studies. This seemed like a good idea to Mona, so she agreed to take the nanny along to America, too.

The next day, Mona met with Dr. Johnson and accepted his offer but told him that she wanted to bring her kids, and her nanny to help with them.

He shook his head and said, "If you bring your nanny along with you, she'll be required to attend classes, and if she's in school, she'll be like a third kid. She also doesn't know the culture. There are babysitters in America, you know, and preschools for your younger child. Besides that, nannies usually leave their employers while overseas because they find jobs or get married." Mona hadn't factored any of these thoughts, not to mention her nanny couldn't even read or write in Arabic, let alone study in English. Mona agreed that since her nanny was also only fifteen, she would leave her in Egypt and just take her two girls as Dr. Johnson had suggested.

Mona officially accepted the offer which meant, while in America, she would work four hours every day in addition to being a full-time student. Her compensation, or student stipend for this, would result in four hundred dollars per month.

The next few months were really busy. Mona had numerous discussions with Dr. Gamal about the project and her concerns with taking her children to a new and foreign land. Not to mention all that she had to prepare for her, and the girls', international travel to the States. The day finally arrived for Mona to leave for America. Her flight was in the evening, and Mona boarded the big jetliner with much excitement, three suitcases, and her two daughters, Yasmeen and Asma.

Welcome to
the USA

Mona set foot on American soil on August 5, 1978. She arrived first at Dulles International Airport in Washington, DC, tired and jet-lagged and toting two equally tired kids. The memory of her last few days in Egypt had been full of visits from, relatives and friends, seeing her off and giving her farewell gifts. Omar and her parents saw her and the girls off at the Cairo airport with tearful good-byes. Everyone was a little frightened, even Mona.

Mona was always up for a challenge, but she didn't realize just how difficult going to a foreign country with two growing children was going to be. As they went through customs, Mona experienced quite a surprise. She wasn't aware that carrying food into the country was prohibited, so all the food they brought was trashed. The kids were scared by this, and the authorities they couldn't understand, and started to cry.

Then they traveled to Montana, arriving just a few weeks before the start of the school year so they had time to get to know Bozeman, the town that was to be their home for the next four years. Mona also needed the time to register for classes and find a place to live. Mona managed to console her children and put them to bed on their first night in the United States in their room at the Henry Manner, which Mona had rented for a few weeks until she could receive accommodations on campus. She had brought an electric plate so she could cook for herself and the kids, and the room had a small refrigerator for storing milk and such. When classes started at the university, Mona took the kids with her every day for the first few weeks.

Mona then had the task of getting her daughters into school and finding affordable accommodations on campus. She lived on her scholarship fund and soon realized that the money she had brought along with her wouldn't buy much. Mona also received a three-thousand-dollar grant from the

Egyptian government to help with expenses which, fortunately, gave her an additional three hundred dollars each month to support her family on top of her four-hundred-dollar stipend.

She eventually found a small two-bedroom apartment, at the Campus Village Apartments where many graduate students lived, for two hundred dollars per month. For Asma, she had found a preschool, which cost three hundred dollars per month. Yasmeen attended a local elementary school at no expense, so Mona had two hundred dollars left over to buy groceries, clothes, and other necessities for the family. Mona was accustomed to a luxurious life back home with a big house, a maid and nanny, and a car with her own personal driver. But, now in the United States, she had to do everything on her own, and knew very few people. She had to make do with a cramped apartment, no maid, and no car. She now had to struggle to make something for herself, and it was not easy.

Mona's biggest problem became transportation. Omar and her father had insisted that she wait until Omar came to buy a car. Omar fancied himself to be a car specialist and was convinced that salesmen would take advantage of Mona and sell her a defective car. This plan, by her mechanical engineer husband, was a big mistake to Mona as she suffered through the first semester without a car, defective or not.

School, for Mona, wasn't turning out to be an easy adjustment either. The coursework was difficult, and in a foreign language to her. Mona had completed her prior education in her native language, Arabic, and although she had learned French and English, her English was quite basic and not sufficient for the advanced coursework that was expected of her right away. Mona wasn't one to give up, though, and she worked extra hard to keep up to speed with her classes.

She found it extremely challenging to decide what to study for each course and how much time to devote to each in turn. The large volume of material she had to learn was also overwhelming. Her aptitude for mathematics made things easier, but she had to work twice as hard as her classmates to maintain her grades because of the language barrier. And although Mona thought the American professors spoke fast, it was nothing compared to the speed of the campus' foreign instructors.

Mona learned to speed up. To save time at home, she dressed the kids for school the night before and let them sleep in their clothes because she had to go directly to class in the morning. She made a friend in her neighbor from Iran who gave her rides to campus, otherwise she managed to walk and bike all over the city of Bozeman.

The kids had their own problems adjusting to their new environment, new school and the loss of their luxuries back in Egypt. But in time, Mona managed to get Yasmeen and Asma to help with the household chores and they eventually got used to this way of life without their Egyptian maids. They had a harder time adjusting to their new school and they struggled to fit in. The other children were cruel to them, as they weren't used to seeing children who looked and spoke like Yasmeen and Asma. The girls came home crying, which was painful for Mona to see as she recalled the racism and prejudice she had seen herself and the devastation it caused. Mona did her best to console her daughters and assure them that things would get better, and that, in time, they would make new friends who saw past their differences.

Before long, Mona had enough of walking and biking and decided to ignore Omar, and her father's advice, and buy her own car. Mona found a Volkswagen Bug for $1,200 that seemed to solve most of her transportation problems. Although she felt Omar would be proud of the purchase she made all on her own, she knew he would never approve of the color . . . lemon yellow.

Mona was accustomed to being a straight-A student with a GPA of 4.0. So when Mona received a 78% on her first test in America, she was particularly disappointed. After all that studying and hard work, she only received a C! Although this was just not acceptable for her, it was the case, as Mona only earned C's on her midterm exams. However, by the end of the first semester, she did much better, and eventually earned A's on her final exams. Mona was most concerned about mastering the material in English. As such, she learned that if she studied with her western peers and asked lots of questions, she'd then begin to understand the lectures.

Graduate school seemed much more challenging for Mona than it was for most of her classmates. Her department provided no special assistance for those who were unfamiliar with English, and Mona was one of only five international students in the department. One student was from India, one from Sri Lanka, another from Indonesia, and one from China, and the five stood out like aliens. Like Mona, they spoke different languages and struggled to understand their professors, their American classmates, and each other.

Furthermore, Mona was the only female student, and she had no female role models in the College of Engineering on campus either. All of the professors were men, as were all of the department heads and deans. Mona felt that they didn't understand how lonely it was to be in a strange land and the only woman in a totally male-dominated educational environment. It also bothered her that they didn't seem to have a clue that women, and other international students, were lacking a sense of belonging and acceptance that often resulted in poor grades. Because if they did relate, or know of the problem, Mona was sure the university would do something about it.

The university offered no mentoring programs for graduate students, or any sort of tutoring or formal study groups. When Mona made the time to meet with her professors outside of class, they always seemed to be too busy with their research. Mona got the impression that the faculty expected graduate students to figure out things by themselves. Mona also felt that some of the professors wondered what she was doing in their classes and whether she could actually even meet their requirements. It was as if they had given up on her. This attitude was familiar to her and made Mona even more determined to prove herself, and so she worked even harder.

During this difficult transition into graduate studies, Mona made a resolution: upon graduating, she would create an environment that would be both welcoming, nourishing and supportive to women and foreign students, wherever she was and in whatever capacity she could.

Outside of study, Mona was busy learning her new culture and English; but English, as it turns out, was a confusing language to her. The slang made it even more disorienting for Mona. Innocent words often came with connotations that she had a hard time understanding. Also, Arabic only had a B in the alphabet. Whereas, English had a B and a P, which made words like "bitch" and "pitch" a challenge among other things. There were other letters, and words, that Mona could also never quite wrap her head around or get correctly. Over the years this made for some comical, and often embarrassing, moments for Mona and the girls.

At one point, she received repeated phone calls from someone she didn't know. It took her quite a while before she understood what was happening. Each time, the caller said things she didn't understand, so she asked him to speak more slowly and to repeat himself in her, now curious, thick accent.

"I'm sorry, but I still don't understand what that word means," Mona finally said. "Can you explain it to me? I don't have the dictionary." The caller happily repeated that he wanted to masturbate and to his surprise, Mona then asked what kind of master's he was pursuing and said that she was working on her PhD.

The caller was incredulous. "You don't know what that means?"

"No, I don't know. Can you explain it to me?" Mona responded.

The caller must have enjoyed their conversation, as he called back several times over the course of her first few months in America. Each time, further broadening her vocabulary with the most colorful words of the English language. Mona eventually learned this to be called "prank-calling". "Prank with a P", Mona proudly had learned.

Life in Montana had begun to form a routine for Mona and the girls. Yasmeen and Asma had made some friends and began to learn the English language proficiently through socializing. Mona fell ill that winter, which concerned the girls, but to everyone's joy and surprise it was just morning sickness. With Omar still in Egypt, on duty, she had to tell him from afar, "I have some news for you, Omar, but I don't want you to worry," Mona went on to say, "It appears I came to the America pregnant, Omar, and we are going to have another baby!"

"Oh, Mona . . . what wonderful news!" Omar said, "I must hurry and get to you and the girls in America." Mona was happy with his response and anxiously awaited her husband's arrival to join them.

Happy Reunion

On November 4, 1979, Iranian militants stormed the United States Embassy in Tehran and took approximately seventy Americans captive. This terrorist act triggered the most profound crisis of the Carter presidency and began a personal ordeal for Jimmy Carter and the American people that lasted 444 days. President Carter committed himself to ensuring the safe return of the hostages while protecting America's interests and prestige. He pursued a policy of restraint that put a higher value on the lives of the hostages than on American power or protecting his own political future. The toll for this patient diplomacy was great, but President Carter's

*actions brought freedom for the hostages and preserved
America's honor.*

Within the year that Mona had left Egypt, Omar
fulfilled his military obligation, resigned from his
post, and set out to join his wife and children in
the United States. President Carter was trying
to negotiate with Iranian militants, and tension
mounted in the United States. Omar's mind was
battling uncertainty and doubt about leaving his
country and starting a new life and a new career
at his age. After rising to the rank of Brigadier
General in the Egyptian army, a prestigious
position that commanded respect, would his job
in the States live up to his expectations? Would he
receive the respect he once had in his homeland?
With these thoughts in his mind, the plane touched
down on foreign soil, and all his doubts vanished
as he set his eyes on his very pregnant wife and
two daughters, who met him at the airport. The
happiness and joy on their faces assured him that
he had made the right decision to come to his
family.

Growing up, Omar became used to a certain
way of life and it was deeply entrenched in the
way he thought and behaved. After a certain point,
these patterns had come to define who he was,
they had become a part of him. Now, in his early
forties, Omar had left behind the country, culture,

and language he had known all his life to start anew. The initial excitement and novelty of being in a new place soon wore off.

Mona had her hands full with the growing baby in her belly, the girls and her schoolwork. She went about her work now with more ease and confidence, which sometimes made Omar feel that he was not well suited for the place. He was still adjusting to the culture whereas she had more time to acclimate to the changes, and that made him feel as if Mona didn't need him. He found the American way of life too impersonal and strange for his comfort. He also had not made any friends yet and often felt that he was at the mercy of his wife. Coming from the male-dominated society of Egypt, in which the man of the house took care of his wife and children, this feeling made him especially uncomfortable.

Omar looked for jobs, but he wasn't satisfied with the offers he was getting, so he decided to go back to school to get his doctorate to bring himself up to speed with the current developments in mechanical engineering. Getting back to school after such a long break was not at all easy for a man of his age. His advisor urged him to brush up on his mathematics before beginning the program so he would be prepared for the advanced study that lay before him.

So, there Omar was, in his early forties and sitting in a class full of youngsters, most of whom spoke good English. After having a position of prestige in college and then later in the army, being a "nobody" in this strange country was depressing for Omar. There were days when he wished he could go back home and have everything the way it was, with his wife and children in his big house and many friends. But as every action has consequences, Omar had no choice but to face his decision and make the best of it.

Omar's turmoil was difficult for Mona. She had been overjoyed at first to see her husband, and thought she'd be relieved to have him with her. She counted on Omar to reduce her burdens of managing the kids, as well as the household, so she could study, but Omar had turned into a completely different person. He complained that he didn't like Montana, that school was difficult, and that he didn't fit in. Omar took his frustrations out on Mona and the kids and lost his temper easily, which was uncharacteristic of him. Mona now felt as though her burdens had suddenly doubled. This was a stressful period. She finally accepted, and hoped, that Omar needed time to adjust, but one year was all she could tolerate to give him. Meanwhile, she continued making progress with her pregnancy and was due any day.

The children were also struggling to adjust to American schools. The Egyptian education system was different than that of America's, and all that Mona and Omar had known. American students were expected to complete many of their tasks at school, with little or no homework. This wasn't acceptable to Mona and Omar, so they constantly asked the girls' teachers for more homework, and this set the girls apart from their classmates. The kids were doing well in school, but for young children, doing well wasn't considered "cool". They had difficulty pleasing their parents while still trying to fit in with their peers.

Over time, the girls kept the taunting to themselves because they didn't want to worry Mona, or upset Omar. They saw how hard their mother worked, and that their father had become harsh and overprotective, a person who yelled when he became angry. They felt the loving and caring father, they once had, seemed to be absent and they didn't want to further upset him. Their parents' constant arguments confused them and began to take a toll on their behavior in class.

The growing pains of the international move brought many challenges and adjustments for each member in Mona's family. It was a time full of joy and sadness, arguments and peace, good grades and bad ones, some laughter and many tears.

Omar's behavior still made Mona's life difficult, and she told him that it was about time he mended his ways, as they were damaging their relationship and the children had noticed.

They finally sat down to talk when the children were away. Mona began, "I understand that you're upset these days, but don't you think you've been taking it too far? Your unhappiness is destroying the peace in our family. If not for me, then for the children, please, try to like where you are and what you're doing. Nothing will come easily if you complain; that only makes our lives miserable. If you really don't like it here, perhaps we should go home and finish our studies there. Otherwise, we can finish our studies and then return home. If you think we should stay on, then you need to change your attitude because I cannot bear it anymore. Should you persist, I think we'll have to go our separate ways."

Omar thought a while and finally said, "I guess I haven't realized how much my unhappiness is affecting everybody. I'm so sorry, Mona. I didn't mean to be this way. We have this great opportunity to study here in America, one of the best places in the world for an education. We shouldn't throw it away; we should take full advantage of our situation. I'll try my best to control my emotions for the sake of my family."

Mona was pleased, and while she focused on her goal of getting A's, Omar focused on his own graduate work, and they agreed they wanted to remain in the United States and finish the year. Mona already knew that she wanted to stay beyond that, but she wasn't sure Omar felt the same way. Mona was optimistic about the vast opportunities available for them, and she was sure that she wanted to raise her children in the American culture, as she knew how difficult it was for females to make their own choices and to control their destiny in the closed culture of the Middle East. She envisioned her children and her grandchildren enjoying the freedom that America had to offer. Mona was also proud of her new home, her new car and deeply grateful for the many opportunities she had found.

Soon after their talk, the university received a grant from the international agency to build an alliance with an Egyptian university and were looking for program directors to guide the oncoming students. The grant allowed two hundred additional graduate students to receive an education in the United States. The Egyptian students were to be welcomed to the country and culture while being mentored during their stay, so the program's administrators called upon Omar and Mona to facilitate a smooth transition for these students and their families.

Omar found himself in a position with the responsibility of arranging the logistics for the students' arrival and catering to their immediate needs. Omar was a natural and became deeply involved in the project. It was an excellent way for him to connect with colleagues from Egypt. To him, nothing seemed better than welcoming his countrymen and making them feel at home in an unfamiliar country that he had started to, now, appreciate.

Just as they found stability again, with Omar's success, the children doing well at school and Mona's progress on her dissertation, there was another big change waiting to take place. By the end of summer, just as the seasons were changing, a handsome, long and healthy baby boy was born. Elated to have a son, their family now felt complete. Mona had chosen the name for their deceased son, Anwar, so she let Omar choose this time. Omar, peering over Mona and his baby boy said, "I am just so happy for your health, and the beautiful family you have given me, Mona. I couldn't ask for anything else, why don't you pick our son's name?" Mona smiled, wrapped the blanket snug around the baby's body, kissed his little forehead and said, "I think we will name him Sammy."

News traveled fast to Egypt, and word of their newborn brought joy to all. Omar and Mona soon had a steady supply of visitors from Egypt, and Omar especially enjoyed the chance to socialize at night, telling jokes in Arabic, watching Egyptian movies, and sharing experiences with new friends. Omar and Mona also felt that their children benefited from the interaction, with the other Egyptian children, as this gave the kids a chance to learn both of their languages and differing cultures.

Life Goes On . . .

Life requires compromise, and Omar and Mona made a few. Mona continued to study, but not without a fight. She put every ounce of her strength and energy into her studies, and she had her share of good and bad days. Mona managed her hardships in her own way, and eventually finished her doctorate in Civil Engineering in 1984 with a GPA of 3.8. Mona's dissertation resulted in a detailed thesis and model of a simulated irrigation system for developing countries. With Mona's model, a farmer could analyze how much water his fields needed based on their soil type, and slope, and decide how best to deliver water to the crops efficiently, which could go a long way toward improving the productivity of the fields. It was a very practical dissertation. Mona applied her model to a local farm in Montana and another in Egypt, and in both cases it worked very well. Mona was happy that her years of work could now contribute to a social cause while assisting farmers.

By the time Mona finished her studies, Omar had finally found his comfort zone, too. He enjoyed the responsibility and the interaction his job afforded him, and he also started making friends to socialize with outside of work. He seemed to be happy and well adjusted for the first time since he had left his country. All in all, it was a good phase in their lives.

Omar and Mona decided that they wanted to remain in the United States permanently. After a rough start, Omar had grown to love the place, and he and Mona both wanted to start the citizenship process. Mona was proud when she became an American, as she now had voting privileges and an American passport. The children kept their Egyptian passports, as they planned to travel back home still and didn't see any real reason to give up their Egyptian papers, but they registered as permanent residents of the United States. The family was not only integrating in America but also considered, now officially, to be part of it.

After Mona graduated, she happened to notice an ad placed for the University of Montana, in Missoula, for a temporary Assistant Professor position in the Department of Physics and Engineering. Mona quickly applied for the job. She learned that the University of Montana originally catered to the educational needs of minority students, and the job was for one year. She visited Missoula for the first time when she went for the interview, and she instantly fell in love with this beautiful little city. It was bigger than Bozeman but had many attractive qualities, including friendly people, a simple lifestyle, and a safe environment. She was offered the position, and she decided that it would provide her a good opportunity for professional development, and Omar agreed.

Mona accepted the position, but it meant that she had to relocate her family once again. As always, her family stood up to the challenge, and Omar and Mona thought it to be more exciting than the children did. Since Yasmeen was in high school, she was most upset about leaving the friends she had worked so hard to make. Asma, who was twelve, was ready for the change as she was more of a loner and wasn't as concern with friends as she was with family. And Sammy, four, wasn't even aware of the family's move to Missoula and therefore had no input on the matter.

Mona settled in and could tell the year was going to be difficult. Mona's teaching load of four courses was demanding for a new professor, but she liked the challenge and the opportunity to prove herself once again. She worked about eighty hours a week preparing for class, teaching, grading papers and exams, and meeting with students during her office hours. One of her highest priorities was good communication with her students. In class, she tried to be very clear and specific and made sure the students understood everything. She found teaching to be rewarding.

She used humor to make up for being different, which the students found endearing. She remembered how hard it was for her to meet with her professors at MSU, so she made sure to be available for her students during office hours. She received fantastic evaluations from her students, as well as other faculty members, and even the department head. They really liked her, and she really liked all of them, too. Although Mona worked such long hours, she was full of energy and enthusiasm as she could see that she made a difference in the classroom. After that wonderful first year, she was offered a permanent faculty position, and she readily accepted it.

Over the summer, Mona returned to Bozeman and MSU to help with the Egyptian alliance project. With her extra income and his continued success, Mona and Omar decided to buy their first condo. Omar was opposed to the idea at first, but Mona convinced him that it would be a good investment and would help cover some of the cost of their daughters' college tuition when the time came.

Omar and Mona concluded that the orientations for the new Egyptian alliance students should also include trips to sites and wonders throughout the United States as part of their tour. Therefore, they visited hydraulics and power facilities in addition to tourist attractions like Disneyland and Las Vegas. Mona and Omar took turns staying home with the kids while the other traveled with, and translated for, the Egyptian visitors. The summer was a happy and productive time for over two hundred Egyptian visitors, and Mona appreciated the opportunity to interact with them for herself and her children.

Mona kept in touch with Celia and Isis, but only Isis was still in Egypt. Celia had moved to the southern region of the United States long before Mona had arrived and was now a happy housewife. She was married to an affluent American doctor named William and they had five wonderful kids. She didn't need to work, so she had a lot of time to keep in touch with their friends from back home in Egypt. If someone was getting married or immigrating, Celia was sure to know about it.

Celia made a special effort to keep tabs on Cohen, over the years, and made it a point to let Mona know of his whereabouts. It had been a long time since Mona had heard anything about him, but finally that summer, Celia let her know that Cohen had moved to the United States and married an American woman. Celia was excited about the news, and Mona was happy to hear about it, but deep within she felt a pang of jealousy. After all these years, she still couldn't understand the hold Cohen had over her. She asked Celia for more information about him in the most inconspicuous manner, as she wanted to know everything—what he did, where he lived, whether he had any children, and anything else Celia happened to know about him. Part of her hoped to see him again someday, but another part refused the idea, as seeing him again would be painful. When it came to Cohen, Mona's mind was in a constant state of conflict.

Upon summer's end, Mona began teaching her second year at the university and she had become even more popular with the students. They loved her class, and she loved to see them smiling while learning. She wanted to make class enjoyable, and she tried her best to speak clearly and prepare neat presentations. Of course, her students found her accent interesting, and their curiosity about it probably attracted them to her class. Mona also tried to be a role model for the few women enrolled in the engineering program.

Mona encouraged lots of discussion in her classes. Once, when the students were negotiating the number of problems they were going to solve, one of the students called his classmate a "brownnoser." Mona didn't have a clue what this meant. Although she was curious, she didn't say anything at the time, but when class was over and she had returned to her office, she looked the word up, but the dictionary wasn't much help. Mona was familiar with the words *brown* and *nose*, but she couldn't find an entry for the combined word. Finally, she asked her own kids when she got home, who provided the definition along with some laughter at her expense. Fortunately, she found that her colleague, Jonathan, was willing to translate American slang into language she could understand, and after that, whenever she was confused about the meaning of something she'd heard, she made a note of it and would ask Jonathan to explain.

One Halloween, Mona found a beautiful white balloon in the corner of her classroom, she picked it up and played with it while she taught. When class was over, she put the balloon on her desk in her office. During the following week, she had many visitors—students, faculty, and even her department chairperson—and all of them seemed to notice the balloon and smile. At the end of the week, Asma, who was about thirteen at the time, came into her office.

"Ma, what is that balloon? Where did you get it from? Why do you have it here?" Asma questioned her mother.

"Isn't it beautiful?" Mona replied.

Asma didn't answer, and didn't waste any time in informing her mother that her new plaything was a condom. Again, Asma, horrified and shocked asks why it was on her mother's desk. Mona was even more curious about how Asma knew what it was! Mona had been married for a long time now, and although she certainly knew what a condom was, she had never seen one blown up and floating around a classroom before. All Mona could think to herself was, "Who knew a condom was so pretty blown up?" Asma explained to her mother that her classmates were known to "borrow" them from their parents for pranks. Of the most popular prank, the kids would fill them with water and throw them at cars. Now all that Mona could think to herself was, "Why do the kids in America throw water condoms at cars for fun?"

Much to the amusement of others, many more comical incidents were yet to come. Mona and Omar handled them with good humor, and tried to learn from them. When, the time came for Mona and Omar to purchase their first condominium, Mona's pronunciation of the word *condo* sounded very much like *condom*, which resulted in some interesting conversations with their real estate agent and banker.

Mona continued practicing Islam in the United States, and this led to more strange encounters when missionaries came to her home to preach the merits of their religions. They seemed to ignore anything Mona said about the issue and continued to preach the "good news," as they called it. They told Mona that she would go to hell if she disagreed, as only belief in Christ secured a way to heaven. Some missionaries invited Mona, and the children, to supper at their churches on the pretext of introducing her to Christianity and ultimately attempting to convert them to Christianity.

Mona believed that God had sent his teachings to the three great religions of Judaism, Christianity, and Islam, and she was raised to believe that Christ was a prophet and not God since, in her view, God was divine and because he wasn't born, he couldn't beget a child. The fact that she believed in Christ and had faith was reason enough, for her, to stick to her beliefs and turn down the missionaries. She believed that every person should have the right to practice their religion without judgment from others, as religious belief was a personal matter for her, Omar and their family.

They were learning that American culture was very different from the more conservative Egyptian culture in other ways, too. Time and money seemed to be the focus of American life, which was different than the culture back home. While Egyptians seemed to focus more on people, the West seemed to be more concerned with money; and Mona had always felt that the people making the money were more important than the money itself.

Family was first in their native land, so the concept of leaving home before marriage, scheduling dates and times to see family, and retiring elders to nursing homes was unheard of, and not very well accepted by Mona and Omar. Family was always welcome in Egypt, and Mona wanted their children to be raised with the same values although in America now. They wanted their children to represent the morals they were instilling in them even though they were learning the American ways, especially at school. When

Mona explained to the girls that a student sitting with his legs up on the chair in front of a teacher would have been inconceivable in Egypt, as the word *professor* was derived from *prophet*, they just laughed.

To Work Is to Worship

During Mona's third year of teaching at the College, it made sense for the family to buy a house rather than a condo. She and Omar looked at twenty-eight houses before they finally decided they had found the perfect home near the mountains, right next to the river. Mona knew that Missoula got a fair amount of snow and she didn't want to be late for her classes, so she liked an old carriage house that was a fifteen-minute walk from campus. It was bright blue, had three bedrooms and was their first real purchase together in America.

As she grew into her new position, she became more involved in the community and developed a good reputation in town. Teachers invited her to middle and high schools to talk to students about their college plans and possible careers in engineering and sciences. By her fourth year, after seeing the need, she began developing outreach programs for middle and high school students and initiated efforts to involve family and community members in educational programs. On campus, Mona was also instrumental in identifying research opportunities for undergraduates and minority students, as she had been one herself once.

Mona continued to interact with community members and students, developing a deeper understanding of the plight of the Native Americans in the area, and beyond. She came from a political knowledge of her country and its region, but was fascinated and excited to learn about America's. This first-hand knowledge with the tribes built on what she had already read about back home when she was studying America in school, but it greatly deepened her compassion for their situation.

It seemed unfair that the original inhabitants of the country felt out of place in their own land. She found her Native American students to be shy and saw that they preferred to be out of the spotlight as much as possible. They seemed awkward and uncomfortable among the other students and when interacting with the faculty, who were mostly white. Moreover, the number of female students was extremely small, and although Mona had seen this among her travels, she was still stunned. Most devastating to Mona was that many of the Native American students dropped out. Mona felt that something needed to be done to make them feel more comfortable so they could take full advantage of the opportunities before them.

She, as a result, started working on a grant proposal for mentoring and tutoring programs so that these college students would be better prepared to take on more advanced studies and be more likely to stay in their degree programs. Mona's strong feelings for this minority population and her own experience as a female engineer, including a lack of mentoring, helped her come up with viable solutions to confront the issues these students faced.

At first, several faculty members were worried about the time Mona spent on grant writing, as they felt that her teaching would suffer as a consequence, but her employers were supportive since they saw that she still fulfilled her teaching responsibilities, and they encouraged her to continue with these endeavors. Mona's proposal was accepted, and the institute received funding. Mona never looked back. Once the grants came in, the faculty realized how beneficial they were. They appreciated the additional opportunity to work with students over the summer, and both faculty and students welcomed the extra income they received from summer research programs.

Mona wrote grants and solicited funds from large corporations to fund these undergraduates, and almost immediately received one hundred thousand dollars from the largest corporation that she approach in 1990, which funded her first summer research program for undergraduates. Encouraged by this success, she wrote another grant for four hundred thousand dollars and was awarded that one as well. This grant provided support for about twenty students to work in research labs each summer.

The students were all hard-working and highly motivated, and all of them graduated. Many of them also gained the confidence and motivation to apply for graduate school or seek jobs in their fields. Thus, the program proved that research for undergraduates encouraged student participation and retention. In addition, through exposure to students of diverse backgrounds, faculty members developed a greater appreciation for cultural differences and brought these new insights to their classrooms.

The next step was to expand the concept to other universities and students throughout Montana, and the nation, to encourage disadvantaged Native American, Hispanic, and female students to pursue majors and careers in science, engineering, mathematics, and technology. After all, what if her children, who are considered minorities, wanted to attend college elsewhere?

Mona solicited support for this ambitious project from colleagues she trusted over the years, and focused her efforts on turning this dream into a reality. She met with presidents, vice presidents, and deans of various colleges to tell them about the merits of the project. Some of them were receptive, but others were less enthusiastic, telling her, "Come and talk to us when you get the money." Mona wondered to herself, again, how money could be more important than these people, these students.

In 1996, Mona received the grant to fund the project nationally and as a result, Mona made many trips to Washington DC to report on the program's progress, and to show that the money was invested well. The three children were grown, with Sammy being the youngest at twelve, so Mona felt she could leave them for her numerous travels. Mona promised the program would double, the number of, minority students who graduated with degrees in engineering and science within five years, and the program met the goal.

As time went by, Mona successfully applied for a number of other grants. She believed that she was progressing toward her goals, but the process was very slow. The percentage of women in engineering was still around 16 percent, and that wasn't enough for her, so she felt she needed to work harder to bring about institutional and cultural change in order to accomplish her goals. She knew such a radical initiative would take a lot of time; to change fundamental cultures and attitudes. Mona dedicated herself to the challenge and remained optimistic that there would be significant improvement in female and minority participation in the sciences within the next decade.

Mona had not forgotten how isolated she felt as a student who didn't understand the dominant language and culture, and additionally didn't feel welcome in a male-dominated environment. She also knew that some women who entered these programs would ultimately find another major and profession if they were not comfortable or endured the same. Yasmeen was attending college in one year and the thought of her daughters in this position, motivated her more than ever.

Bringing the Children Up

Missoula had a wonderful tradition at Halloween: the entire downtown would close to traffic for a street party. Everybody dressed up in costumes and came out to talk to each other, eat, dance and generally have a great time. Since Mona's students took the event very seriously, they often discussed what they were planning to wear, or do, for Halloween. In one class, Mona asked a student what he was going to wear for Halloween, and he responded that he was planning to dress up as an orgasm. She didn't understand what he meant, so when she went home and consulted the resident language expert, her teenage daughter, Asma.

"It can't be!" Asma said. "People can't wear an orgasm as a costume. He can't just go out and make noises in the street!" She thought it was hilarious that Mona didn't know the word and sarcastically wondered exactly how long her mother had been married. Mona was shocked that her students were comfortable discussing such matters with her but more alarmed about what her children were learning, and what Omar would do if he knew.

So, in addition to getting better at the English language, Mona was still adjusting to the cultural differences between her native country and the United States. She had learned to be patient and take things one day at a time. Although she appreciated the opportunities available to her and her family in the United States, she also tried to preserve her Egyptian culture and Islamic traditions.

She taught her daughters of the Five Pillars of Islam: *shahada*, the devoted belief in the Creator; *salat*, the prayer ritual performed five times a day; *sawm*, the fast during the sacred month of Ramadan; *zakat*, alms-giving; and the *hajj*, the sacred pilgrimage to Mecca that all Muslims strive to make at least once in their lives.

The girls also learned that Muslims recognized Jesus Christ as a prophet, and also believed that he would return to earth. As a prophet, Jesus was a messenger and link between the Creator and human beings. To Muslims, the relationship with Allah was very private, and they believed that nobody should be forced to worship. Mona believed that Islam was open to new ideas, and she admired that it was a religion that emphasized on education, critical thinking, and creativity while obliged one to help other people. She had also been taught that people should have mercy for other people on earth so that Allah would have mercy on them in death.

Although Mona appreciated the many positive aspects of the Islamic tradition, she recognized some negative aspects as well. For one thing, some Muslim men were chauvinistic and discriminated against women, as they believed that women should obey them and weren't their equals. She also disagreed about wearing the veil, although many Muslim women accepted the idea, she believed that the Five Pillars of Islam governed behavior and not clothing, and she hadn't been raised in a family that wore the veil. Instead, Mona strongly believed that all people should dress professionally and be comfortable.

Although the children were learning two cultures, Mona instilled the important concepts of Islam as she understood them and the practices she had been raised to follow, including the traditions of prayer, compassion, and fasting. Mona also visited Egypt every three or four years with one or two of the kids so they could become familiar with their family's culture, food, styles of communication, and language.

During Ramadan, Mona's family fasted in order to appreciate the plight of people who didn't have money for food. The fast is for thirty days, from sunrise to sunset and then a big family feast at dusk. Of course, because they had low energy during the day, Mona's family members would only fast if they were well and able.

Mona's parents had also taught her to respect other religions, and growing in a neighborhood with friends who were Coptic Christians and Jews made that easy. Besides, they were very nice people and respected our religion and culture as well. If Mona's family were fasting for Ramadan, for example, their Coptic friends wouldn't eat in front of them, and Mona's family also wouldn't eat meat in front of their Coptic friends during Lent to be sensitive to their beliefs.

In Egypt, as in many developing countries, personal relationships held the highest priority and were more important than money. Mona already knew that she disliked the emphasis on materialism she found in the United States, where time was money and people sometimes focused more on their financial wealth than their personal relationships. Back home in Egypt, people worked and earned a living, of course, but the people's primary focus was on each other, particularly their families.

Mona taught her children to take the best of both of their cultures. In her view, Egypt was like a mother, as a person couldn't choose their mother, and the United States was like a spouse, as a person chose who to marry, and both were wonderful in their own way. Although she hadn't chosen her mother country, she respect it, and she even spoke with respect about the aspects she didn't agree with. But, of course, the children were young and subject to powerful peer pressure. They did not always appreciate their parent's culture because they were confused between their peers' actions and what their parents were saying at home, and the conflicting views.

In Mona's family, she was the communicator and had a softer approach than Omar, who was stern and could still be overprotective and hard to deal with at times. The kids sometimes resented him because he tended to say no to what they wanted to do. When Yasmeen wanted to go to her high school prom, a big fight erupted in the house. Because of how Mona and Omar were raised, Omar didn't believe in prom and, naturally, didn't want her to go on a date with a boy. He was very worried that his daughter might get into trouble because her peers would engage in drinking and sex, issues common for teens in the west, but new to them. Mona finally convinced him to let Yasmeen go, but this argument and those about similar issues created tension in the family as the girls got older. Mona tried her best to balance the children's requests and her husband's wishes, but it was sometimes extremely hard and, for Mona, a real challenge.

These arguments reminded Mona of her own father and their relationship. And she saw the similarities to Ishmael's reaction at the beginning of her relations with Omar. Ishmael was very important in her life, as he was the one person who had really shaped her thoughts and opinions, and she looked up to him. He had encouraged her to push herself to the best of her abilities. Unfortunately, in 1987, Mona's father had passed away in Cairo. Before that, he had come to America almost every year with Mona's mother to visit her family. Ishmael, and Fatma, were always happy to visit, as they saw Mona's progress and watched their grandchildren grow. Ishmael's death was very difficult for the entire family, especially Mona's mother and sisters, who were still in Egypt. Although it had been a few years since his death, Mona was still mourning the loss of her beloved father.

Omar's Entry into the Workforce

Bill Clinton, the forty-second president of the United States, was in office from 1993 to 2001. His most enduring legacy was the economic boom that began in 1992, shortly before he took office, as it brought the country benefits across the income spectrum. President Clinton believed that it took courage to start something new, to carve a dream into reality, especially if one had few resources and lived in difficult circumstances and an economy that demanded much of its participants. He fought to improve the economic security of small businesses by nurturing and supporting the powerful economic engine of the small business sector through policies of fiscal responsibility and wise investment, and he most notably improved access to capital. After President Clinton signed the Small Business Lending Enhancement Act, the number of loans made under its cornerstone 7(a) Guaranteed Business Loan Program more than doubled, increasing from twenty-seven thousand loans in 1992 to fifty-seven thousand in 1995.

In the early nineties, Mona was established at work, the children had settled in school, and Omar had also received his doctoral degree in mechanical engineering by now. His family and friends were very happy for him as this was always his dream, and a difficult feat. Mona threw a cozy party and invited a few friends to celebrate this big milestone. However, Omar's happiness and joy was short-lived when he tried his luck in the job market.

Day after day, Omar applied for jobs, posting his resume wherever he could. Then he waited. The waiting became unbearable, without even a single call for an interview. It became evident that because of his age, he wasn't employers' first choice. As time went by, his patience was tested to the limits, and he became frustrated and bitter. Such excellent qualifications seemed to be of no use to him in this country. When he applied for a post as a professor in a college, he was rejected because of his heavily accented English. Mona's English was better as she had more time in the states and more practice, than Omar, through her students and classes. To add to matters, he couldn't enter the commercial scene, as prospective employers denied him claiming that he was overqualified but hiring his equally qualified classmates who were fifteen to twenty years younger.

It was clear that he was being discriminated against because of his age. When this well-accomplished, energetic man had to sit at home against his wishes, neither he nor the people close to him could be happy. Watching Mona go to work every day and be so successful was something he had been proud of, but now as the proud man he was, it bothered him. Yasmeen was now away at college, and Asma and Sammy were busy with extracurricular activities. Omar was alone and at home most of the time which made matters worse. Omar and Mona had to decide as a couple what they were going to do. For the second time during their stay in the United States, they had to reach an agreement about how to save their relationship and restore Omar's injured self-confidence.

Finally, Omar and Mona concluded that they needed to create a job for Omar. They envisioned the family working together in Missoula, and they found that opportunity in a place called Joe's

Auto, a cute auto shop in a good location, that sold used cars and repaired vehicles. A perfect job for a physically able, mechanical engineer with a doctorate. Plus, with Omar's sense of humor, and joke skills that he had now carried over to English, it seemed a good fit. Omar was a little more cautious and less optimistic about the endeavor than Mona, who, being the go-getter that she was, thought it was a great opportunity for the family.

She saw them all working there together, with Omar as the owner and the children learning the business and running the office. Mona said she was willing to work there after school for a year or two, and this finally convinced Omar. In the coming few months, Omar kept busy meeting with people to work out a feasible plan. Then, in early 1993, Omar and Mona borrowed money to purchase the auto shop, which they renamed Ramsey's Auto.

The business took off, and the family did very well. Now in control of his own business and working as his own boss, Omar was the happiest man of his time. Mona was busy at the college, but when she got off work in the evenings, she spent time in the auto shop interacting with guests, scoping out new cars for herself, and helping with financial matters. Sammy also came down to the auto shop to help whenever he had time, which happened to be most of the time, as he enjoyed the work and the interactions with people that it offered, much like his father. They met an array of people, whom they often helped, as Omar had a soft spot for those less fortunate and could arrange financing or slash prices, if he deemed.

Mona learned about cars; but more, from talking to the customers, about all kinds of other things. The work provided her a change of pace from her day job, and she found it to be a stress reliever. Missoula probably wasn't big enough for her big ambitions, so Mona was glad for these new responsibilities to channel her energy and keep her busy, especially since the children had started lives of their own. She also loved to see Omar busy and animated. It was just like the old days. Mona found the business relaxing, and she like that she could enjoy life with her family and clients and still make money. The auto shop continued to be successful and earned good revenue, so Mona thought it would be a good idea to expand and buy a second business. Omar disagreed.

So the couple continued to focus on their, one, successful business. They employed mostly students through business and mechanical internships, and saw this as yet another way to serve the community and colleges. In addition, Sammy, who now served as the auto shops' general manager, was gaining valuable job experience, making good money and attaining skills. Mona and Omar valued the family's success together. All in all, she felt happy and content as things fell into place over the years.

The Empty Nest

Yasmeen, Mona and Omar's eldest daughter, went to MSU and successfully graduated with degrees in finance and marketing. Asma went to the University of Montana for one year and then transferred to University of California, Berkeley. Sammy, the youngest, still lived in Missoula, was attending college and ran the auto shop with his father.

Yasmeen and Asma had faced a lot of problems in high school. They smoked cigarettes, ditched class, and experienced with alcohol, which greatly upset Mona. Omar was a smoker, but Mona hated smoking and the smell of cigarettes. Smoking had been fashionable when Mona was young, for both men and women, but the habit never attracted her. Yasmeen and Asma both started smoking around the age of twelve, but Mona didn't find out about it until later because they hid it very well.

Yasmeen always looked out for Asma, but one day it seemed they just stopped getting along. Cultural differences with their classmates, peer pressure, and the high expectations from the family affected the kids deeply. All of them suffered the consequences, but for Asma they seemed worst. She turned to her studies and read many books. With the exception of her pet, Cleo the cat, she spent most of her time alone. Asma struggled with addictions, alcohol in particular, and eventually she turned to Mona for help. Asma had been arrested for drinking and driving while in her first year of college and the incident revealed the substance abuse that was so well hidden from Mona and Omar. After treatment, Asma's only vice was cigarette smoking and coffee, but Mona still persistently pushed for her to quit tobacco.

Yasmeen had always been rebellious and enjoyed the party atmosphere and the people that came with it. She had a social, funny nature just like Omar's and fit in well as she had fair skin and spoke perfect English. Like many other students, for her, college life meant boys, alcohol and fun.

Although Mona disapproved, she knew that many college students had, since time, the same idea and she realized that Yasmeen would outgrow those habits. Or, at least, Mona hoped.

Sammy had been raised entirely in the United States, so his adaption to the culture of his adopted country was subtler. He did have some health problems when he was young, however. But, gradually, he got better and stronger and resembled Omar in his apt for physical strength. He loved camping, the mountains, skiing, mountain biking, the river and horses. He had two by the time he was twenty, Otis and Sebastian, and took care of them well. Missoula was home and he didn't want to leave. Although this pleased Mona, to have her baby close by, she just wished he would marry and produce grandchildren.

All three children did well in school, and Mona and Omar were proud that their smart, beautiful kids graduated and pursued good careers. When Yasmeen finished her degree in finance, she took a job in Manhattan. Mona visited her there but felt it unsafe from the moment she stepped outside the airport. Mona also didn't like how expensive the city was, and knew how little her daughter was making her first year in the corporate world. Perhaps she just wanted her daughter closer to home, regardless, Mona hated New York upon arrival.

On the trip from the airport to Yasmeen's apartment, the taxi driver overcharged Mona, which was definitely not the best way to make a good impression on a visitor. Yasmeen paid a thousand dollars in rent, each month, for an apartment so small that there wasn't even a sofa for Mona, or another guest, to sleep on. Mona stayed in a hotel. The cramped room cost two hundred dollars per night and had cockroaches.

Every time she made a phone call, she was charged a dollar, even if the call didn't go through. By the end of her stay, Mona owed over thirty-five dollars for phone calls that weren't answered, or ever made. When she complained, the management explained that this was hotel policy and was displayed everywhere in the room. Turns out, the warnings were printed in small letters behind the door, where nobody would ever notice them. Mona got the feeling that everybody in New York dedicated their lives to stripping others of their money. And they were rude, to boot.

Mona asked Yasmeen, "How can you possibly live here?" Yasmeen responded, "I like it, Mom. It's a great experience and I'm trying something new." Yasmeen was brave, braver than Mona who couldn't wait to leave.

For her second year of college, Asma went to California, sober, for a biology degree at Berkeley. Her training led her instead into the veterinary program which was fitting since she loved animals. It was a lot of work, but she was successful, and she eventually found a job in an animal hospital in San Diego. She worked there for a while and then took another position in San Francisco. Although she found a well-suited career, California wasn't a good match. Eventually, she returned to Bozeman and took a job with two local vet practices, both part time. With the extra time she had, she would assist on ranches in the area, and was able to work with large animals, too.

Sammy majored in mechanical engineering and business at the University of Montana and continued to run the family business with Omar. They got along great, and the town knew them as a pair not to contend with. Business was good and they were making good money and lifelong friends. Sometimes however, when you're young, making too much money can be a bad thing. Sammy discover drugs in the nightclub scene which was abundant, for Montana, because of the many colleges. After his addiction to cocaine, he lost the good friends he made growing up and most of his possessions.

The addiction was ugly, strong and controlled Mona's son. She could not relate as she had never been addicted to anything her whole life. It truly hurt her to watch the travesty, but until he lost his horses to the drug, he did not see the severity of his problem. With no money, job (Omar tried tough love with his son), friends or hope, Sammy turned to his parents for help. This addiction was harder, it seemed to Mona, than alcohol, but Sammy was tough and managed to finish the treatment and become and advocate and mentor for others.

After her stint in New York, Yasmeen went to Japan to travel and work for a foreign bank. Mona thought it to be a wonderful experience, for Yasmeen, to learn another language and to live overseas while getting paid. Mona, too, went to Japan for a month to visit, and she enjoyed the Japanese culture, food, and people, whom she found to be generous, hospitable, and fun to be around. For the first time in her life, she felt like a giant at five feet tall. Even though she wore heels all the time, Mona was shorter than the average American. In comparison to most Japanese women, though, she was really tall in her mind. In contrast to New York, Japan felt safe and friendly and she was happy that Yasmeen had moved.

Yasmeen's passport expired while she was in Japan, and she was told that she had to go to the United States or to an embassy in another country and return with her passport renewed. So she went home to the United States, stayed with her parents, and took a temporary position with an investment brokerage in Bozeman. There, she met a young man from California named Charlie, who fell in love with Yasmeen the minute he saw her. He wanted to marry her, but she wasn't interested. "I'm not here to get married," she said. "I'm only here until I obtain a new passport, and then I'll go back to Japan."

But Charlie was persistent. He invited her to dinner and brought her gifts. He showed Yasmeen he was generous, loving, and caring. She brought him around to meet Omar and Mona, and Mona fell in love with him the minute she saw him. She thought that he would be a good son-in-law, but, of course, Omar had a different reaction. Like other overprotective fathers, he didn't think that any man would be good enough for his daughter. He behaved just as Mona's father had many years before, and Yasmeen knew he would.

Charlie insisted, "I don't want anything from you Yasmeen; I just enjoy your company. I'll be happy with whatever decision you make."

Eventually, Yasmeen's passport was renewed and she returned to Japan, alone.

Mona was grateful for her children's inclusion in their lives and the place in life they had finally found. She had learned a lot from them, especially through their experiences and challenges. Yasmeen, Asma and Sammy reflected her and Omar's qualities, both good and bad, and she was proud of them. Most of all, they were her strength.

Chance Encounter

Work went on smoothly for Mona, and she continued writing proposals and developing grants successfully. It also provided her with opportunities to travel around the country to present her goals and ideas, which suited her well, as she enjoyed seeing and experiencing new places. While she was away, she left Omar in charge, which was much easier now that the children were adults and busy with their own lives.

The opportunities to travel and share her ideas, and the freedom that Western culture permitted, made Mona love the United States all the most. The hardest part of her job seemed to be the firsthand discrimination she saw that Native Americans, Hispanics, and African Americans faced through her interactions with her students and their families around America. This motivated her to work harder to make a difference in their lives, and her passion to reach out to these underprivileged people increased.

Mona traveled to Chicago for a conference that addressed the needs of the underprivileged populations who were underrepresented in higher education. She received accolades for her contributions in the field, and attendees applauded her presentation, making Mona feel that her efforts were worthwhile after all these years.

As she walked offstage, the corner of her eye caught an impression of a face she believed she'd seen before. She tried to spot it again through the crowd as her memory thought she saw someone in the audience who looked familiar. The gentleman had a broad smile, a big nose and receding, but thick jet-black hair. She thought he looked like Cohen, but then she laughed to herself for imagining things. She shook the thought off instantly and, with a little guilt, returned to her colleagues.

Later in the evening at the academic reception party, she heard someone call her name. "Mona!" A man's voice shouted from behind her. She turned around to find herself the recipient of a hug from the same guy she had early thought familiar. Cohen, who she had been trying to get out of her mind all evening, all her life, was tightly embracing her.

"Mona! How have you been?" Cohen said when he finally let go. "You look well. Your presentation was amazing."

Mona stood as still as a block of ice; too shocked to move. When she finally got over her initial surprise, all she could manage to say was, "You look good too." She felt embarrassed the moment the words left her mouth and tried to recover the slip by saying, "I mean, thank you. It's nice to see you!"

She couldn't believe that after all these years, she was seeing this man (whom she still dreamt about) in the flesh. All the emotions she had pent up over the years suddenly came to the surface, and she still couldn't acknowledge them. The heat in her body began to rise, her palms felt clammy and her heart pulsed with intensity that could be heard in the deep of her ear. Mona was rarely at a loss for words or ever nervous, but Cohen had made her both.

She finally regained her composure, and the conversation flowed as though they had never been away from each other. They talked about everything: how life had turned out for both of them, how they had ended up in the United States, and about their careers, their marriages, their children, and how things were going in general.

Cohen had married an American, which Mona knew thanks to Celia, but what she didn't know was that the marriage was failing. Cohen had two children and was making efforts to salvage his marriage for their sake, but he focused most of his energy on his work as a software engineer with a good firm in Chicago. He shared the same passion as Mona for enhancing diversity, and he worked closely with his company's human resources department to do so. This was a cause close to his heart because he had been discriminated against all his life for being Jewish as well as an Egyptian.

It suddenly felt as though they were back home in Egypt in that little, dusty, narrow alley putting their scooter together. Much like then, they were laughing, learning and loving the time together. When the conference ended, Cohen and Mona exchanged contact details and agreed to stay in touch, and they returned to the realities of their lives.

Mona returned home but felt as though she had left a part of herself with Cohen. She seemed disinterested and lost, and she thought of how things would have turned out had she decided to settle down with Cohen instead of Omar. She knew that was never possible, but yet she couldn't stop herself from thinking about Cohen.

Mona had her head in the clouds after seeing Cohen in Chicago for several days upon returning home. All it took was a phone call from Celia to abruptly bring her back to her senses. Celia was in distress. Her marriage to William was failing. They had fallen in love at first sight when they met each other at a Coptic wedding in Egypt. After a whirlwind engagement, they married according to her customs and traditions.

William earned enough money in the United States to allow Celia to dedicate all her time to her home and their children, while he spent increasing amounts of time at work. Celia didn't suspect anything was wrong, thinking that the long hours were part of his job. However, he came home one day and announced that he had found somebody else, the nurse at his workplace. He was having an affair and leaving Celia and the kids. Celia was still young and attractive and could easily find somebody to replace him, but couldn't see around the thought that he was abandoning her for a younger, more beautiful woman.

He agreed to compensate Celia financially, as well as the children's needs, because he had acquired a fair amount of money and riches in their time together. The children would soon leave for college and be on their own, and he felt that money could fix any problem, even marital. Celia believed that he was trying to buy her and the kids off and it only made her resent him more. She put up a tough fight and made the legal process hard for him, as it was the only thing she had any control of.

Celia was completely shattered. Mona could barely understand her through her sobbing and wailing. She was hysterical and inconsolable when she called Mona with the news. Although Mona tried to comfort her, Celia's conservative Coptic Christian background didn't help, as it had instilled in her a commitment to her marriage vows and taught her that they weren't to be taken lightly. Maybe that's why Celia had such a hard time letting go of William, or even fathoming it.

Mona invited Celia to her home to spend time away, hoping a change of environment would take her mind off the memories in her house. They had been best friends for life and it was a good time as they acted just like schoolgirls again. Mona reluctantly shared the news that she had met Cohen hoping it would take Celia's mind off things for a bit, but it didn't elicit the response she had expected from Celia.

"I did things the right way," Celia said. "I married a person I loved dearly. I gave him five beautiful children, and I took care of his home. Where did I go wrong? There is absolutely no way of knowing when a marriage could fall apart and leave you with nothing." As if staring directly into Mona's core, with an attacking voice, Celia barely takes a breath and continues, "If you think Cohen would have made your life different, don't believe it. I suggest you make your peace with what you have at the moment. You have a man who dotes on you and your three children. You work and do what makes you happy. What more do you want from life? Focus on what is, rather than what could have been, Mona. You never know when you might lose what you have."

Mona realized that Celia wasn't in her usual frame of mind, as she spoke to Mona so forcefully and out of anger and resentment, so she did not say anything in retaliation. Mona realized that Celia was really telling her that she should purge her feelings for Cohen, at last and forever. Mona knew she was right as she, too, believed that they could only cause trouble for everyone involved.

Mona decided she dare not tell Celia that she had been in secret communications with Cohen, over the phone, almost every day since Chicago. She rather, contemplated the conversation with Celia and her lifelong fantasies of Cohen and knew she had to make contact with him immediately.

She decided that he could only have a place in her life as a friend and that she needed to tell him. It was not that easy. Over the course of their reconnection, Cohen had rediscovered the depth of his feelings for Mona and had expressed them to her. Reluctantly, she persisted that he understand how she felt and hoped he'd agree to maintain a friendship. Cohen eventually succumbed to the idea. They maintained a correspondence, telling each other of the happenings of their lives and work and about opportunities to meet each other at professional events. Despite all her resolve to consider him as nothing more than a friend, Mona's feelings for him only got stronger with time.

Rude Awakening

Mona always loved Omar, Cohen had not swayed her before, and she wasn't about to let him now. After Mona's conversation with Cohen, her focus shifted back to her life with Omar. A life she realized that she adored. Mona fully embraced Montana's riches with a good business, career, friends, a home, a beautiful garden and Omar and thought she was in heaven. But it felt as God were playing a cruel trick on Mona, for just as she learned to enjoy the love she shared with Omar, and be content with her happiness that few were as lucky to see in a lifetime, it came to a quick halt.

In 2000, on the last day of a family vacation, Omar woke up early, had a shower, ate a small breakfast, and lay on the couch to watch TV, while Mona and the children were still asleep. He often got up in the night as war made it hard for him to sleep, but this night was different. It seems, without warning, Omar suffered a heart attack so severe that when Mona woke up her husband was not breathing. Omar had died in his sleep a few hours before Mona found him. In that moment, she felt alone with three children, her career, the garden, the pets, the bills, the families and, unfathomably for her to imagine, a business to also take care of.

Mona was in complete shock, as were the children, as it happened so fast and without warning. One moment they were happy and laughing, and the next moment their lives had changed as though lightning had struck. The incidents that followed were, to Mona, a blur, as her mind couldn't register the loss she had just endured. She felt she had to put on a brave face for the sake of her children, which made the situation all the more difficult for her. Mona and the girls buried Omar in Bozeman and began their emotional and financial adjustments. Just being alone in the house was now hard for Mona because she had not been alone in many years. She raised three children, hosted many parties and gatherings and at least had the sound of Omar's television echoing in the background, that the silence was numbing to her. As now, all the children were gone and so was Omar. Mona was all alone.

Celia, having recovered from her loss, came to visit and help Mona through this time of crisis. She was a major source of encouragement and support for Mona. Mona was so engulfed in grief that she lost any, and all, sense of joy. She just took each day as it came for the sake of her children, and tried not to think too far ahead. Celia was helpful to have around although it wasn't the jolly time that their usual reunions were.

Cohen heard about Mona's loss and offered his support, from afar, as well. He did whatever he could to assure Mona that she didn't feel alone. He sent flowers and cards and called regularly to check that she was eating well and getting enough rest. When Mona wouldn't answer he would call Celia to assure she was doing okay. Cohen knew Mona would immerse herself in work to drown her sorrows, but he was concerned that she would burn out and fall ill as a result of taking care of her many obligations on her own. Celia eventually returned home, and so had the children, so Mona was in Montana alone. Cohen lent Mona an ear whenever she needed him, but he wished she'd let him do more to support her.

She couldn't understand why this had happened to her, as she had neither hurt nor wronged anybody. Mona recalled that Celia felt this way when Mona went to help comfort her through her divorce. The same utter hopelessness and loneliness they now had in common. Did her guilty thoughts of Cohen have anything to do with what had happened? Was she being punished for having a secret relationship with Cohen, even though she never acted on it? Mona went through these phases several times before she finally accepted her fate, and was ever grateful for the help of her friends and family.

This was one of the most difficult times in Mona's life, but the experience only added to her strength and she began to bounce back. Being strong willed, Mona was able to overcome her grief, pull herself together, and move on. Although it didn't happen overnight, it became easier each day.

It took Mona five years to adjust back to normal. The first three years were the most difficult. Mona didn't make any immediate changes, as her friends advised her not to make decisions when she was sad or angry. She was both, but most angry that Omar had passed away unexpectedly, and everything that reminded her of him made her angry: the auto shop, her jewelry, even her soap.

Mona learned to take everything one day at a time, but because of her anger, she couldn't plan ahead and often didn't know what to do. She relied on the help of her children to decide what was best to do with the business, as life in Missoula was difficult for her now that Omar was no longer a part of it. Sammy kept a close eye on his mother and agreed to continue managing the auto shop while still finishing his college education.

After about a year, Mona began to notice the affects the work load and grief were taking on Sammy, so she approached the children and asked if they would be alright with the idea of selling their father's business. The family collectively decided to sell the auto shop and they listed it with the area's best agent. Fortunately the shop sold quickly and, with the proceeds, she managed to pay off the loan and consolidate what she had so she could be comfortable.

Mona moved outside of Bozeman, largely to get away from the memory of Omar, but she kept her position in Missoula, as her job had always been important. Mona started over—she bought a new house, new furniture, and even fun new toys, including a plasma TV and a shiny, new, hot-red car that was fully loaded. Life was getting back to normal. A new normal for Mona.

A New Start

Mona's move outside the city was one of many changes in her life. To begin with, Yasmeen and Paulo moved in with her. Paulo was a charming short, balding Argentinian man who spoke with a thick accent and loved to cook. He was also Mona's new son-in-law, as Yasmeen and he had been married the year before in Japan where they met. Although this was the first acquaintance for her with Paulo, Mona fell for his Latin charm from the start.

Mona was grateful for their presence, as they kept her from feeling lonely, and the young couple could save some money at the same time.

Yasmeen was pregnant when they moved in. Nobody knew at the time, as she wasn't showing and they hadn't planned for a child. Everyone was ecstatic, especially Mona who was going to be a grandmother for the first time.

The couple didn't want to know the gender of the child, but Mona did since she had two girls and wanted one more boy. Yasmeen and Paulo allowed her to ask the doctor the sex of her first-born grandchild, only if Mona promised to keep it a secret. Although, in the coming months, they tried to trick Mona into telling them many times, she never let them know it was a girl.

"C'mon, Mama, what do you think? Should I pick pink hues or blue for the nursery? I need your input because you're the grandmother," Yasmeen once asked with a mischievous wink.

Since Mona didn't seem enthusiastic (as she would have had the baby been another boy), the young coupled guessed that their baby must be a girl. Sure enough, Carmen was born nine months after Omar passed away. One look at her pretty grandchild was enough to put Mona's dejection at not having a grandson aside! However, she couldn't stop thinking about how Omar hadn't learned of Yasmeen's pregnancy before he died, and how happy he would be now.

Yasmeen and Paulo stayed with Mona for the next ten months after Carmen was born. Ten wonderful months for Mona. At night, Mona had her granddaughter to play with, and Paulo, the great cook—too good for Mona's waistline, was always making magic in the kitchen. The house was full of noise, aroma, family and hope.

The sounds of a full house and the smell of food cooking were good distractions, but Mona still thought of Cohen every now and then. Particularly when he would call to check on her. This was a period of recovery for Mona, and her grandbaby helped her collect the pieces of her broken heart and slowly grow strong again.

Eventually, Yasmeen, Paulo and baby Carmen moved out and Mona's old fears returned. Mona had never lived alone until now, and was nervous about it. When the wind blew, she thought someone was knocking on the door, and when the house creaked, she thought there was an intruder. Cohen finally persuaded her to have a security system installed in order to ease her discomfort, but even with the system, a minute and a half elapsed between the system's notification and the police's arrival, and the idea of that minute and a half alone with an intruder was in the back of her mind at all times.

Yasmeen and Paulo, to her relief and joy, moved very close to Mona. Asma worked as a veterinarian in her own hospital in Bozeman and also decided to buy her own house, as she was still single and doing very well for herself. Mona was still excelling at her job, but she was tired of her monotonous routine, and coping with boredom proved difficult. These challenges were different from those she had faced in the Middle East, and though life wasn't easy, it was manageable in her mind.

Sammy was glad to have the weight of the auto shop off his shoulders and was glad that Mona had Carmen to pamper. Being the mountain enthusiast that he was, Sammy continued living in Missoula and became a professional mountain bike racer. Mona was very happy that her son was pursuing his dreams, even though she worried about injury, she was glad for his health and achievements. Although he had plenty of women around, too many in Mona's opinion, he hadn't found anyone to settle down with yet. He visited Mona in Bozeman as much as he could, but the visits were short, as Sammy was always very busy training or racing.

Cohen in Crisis

Life is a rollercoaster. Just as things were beginning to look up for Mona, Cohen was headed downhill. His personal life was an utter mess. He had worked hard to make his marriage work for the sake of his children, but now that the children were away at college, the marriage was disintegrating fast.

According to Celia, Cohen's wife was seeing somebody else and found Cohen to be a complete bore. She thought he lacked color and was making her life colorless as well. She insisted on a separation, and Cohen granted it. Mona was happy that Celia had called her with this information, but she wondered if Cohen was okay. Mona decided to call, so she picked up the phone, immediately after hanging up with Celia, and dialed Cohen's number. After three rings, Cohen answered her call.

Mona with great concern started, "Hi Cohen, how are you? Is there anything I can do?" Mona knew he would have called by now if he needed her, but she wanted him to know she was there for him and that she cared. "Mona?" A faint and sad Cohen replied. "Yes, Cohen. It's Mona. I would have called sooner, I'm so sorry, I just found out . . ." Cohen interrupted and said, "I'll be okay Mona, I have recovered from a greater loss once before, so I should make it through this just fine." Mona felt the sharp tone of his words and she knew what he was referring to, but she didn't say anything in response. Instead, Mona tried to stay positive and let him feel the anger he had towards his ex-wife and towards her.

Having gone through a similar situation, Celia tried to make Cohen understand that not all was lost, as it was never too late to find true love. She reminded him that he would probably find it in the most unexpected way and be happy again. Mona, too, knew what he felt, so she empathized with Cohen and give him moral support whenever he sought her advice.

In spite of all Cohen's efforts, his marriage ended in divorce. With a heavy heart, Cohen signed the papers and released his wife. He was now all alone. Thankfully, Mona was in contact with him on a more regular basis and they were both learning to live alone.

Soon after his divorce, Mona ran into Cohen at a class reunion, in Vail, Colorado, for all of the Egyptian engineers who had attended university together in Cairo. Seven of them now lived permanently in America and they decided to meet, at a lodge, in the mountains. When Mona laid eyes on Cohen, a rush of feelings swept over her. When she first encountered him at the airport (they both landed before the group) she examined every detail of his being as he walked toward her.

Cohen was still handsome, professional, and well mannered. Everything about him was composed. He was perfectly ironed while sloppy, and composed but passionate. It was as if he never spoke without thorough contemplation, as he always said the right thing at the right time. He was just as Mona remembered him, and just a bit more refined.

The instant chemistry that they had shared years before still existed now that they were face-to-face. All the phone conversations in the last few months made dialogue easy, and Mona flirted, as did Cohen. It was a good sign. He told her, repeatedly, that she looked the same as she did when she was sixteen. She found Cohen somehow more charming, although she didn't tell him. They were lost in each other.

Unfortunately, the rest of the group finally arrived. They took an eight-passenger van to Vail. The drive was a lot of fun as everyone discussed where they were coming from and their excitement to meet and reconnect after thirty years. They spoke English but occasionally threw in bits of Arabic. Mona took on the role of the tour guide, explaining the mountains and attractions of Colorado, as she had been there once before.

Mona felt alive and much younger than she was. The group had aged, some better than others, and they had decades to catch up on since they were in college. No spouses were allowed on the trip and, of the seven-member group, Celia and Mona were the only women. Everyone had a different personal situation, and the one thing they had in common was that they were all successful in their careers. John was married to an American and was working in the industry; he had no children. Kamel flew in from Washington, DC. He was married and had two children who were already through college. He told the group that his wife made more money than he did, which clearly made him uncomfortable and caused strife in their marriage.

Tarek was a very successful engineer and he, too, was having problems with his wife because his impressive career took up all of his time. He had been a bit of a workaholic as a teenager, too—he never stopped studying. Tarek's wife had threatened divorce, and their children were still in high school. Of all the engineers on the bus, he was still, by far, the biggest geek in our group.

Celia said that she was trying to forget her marriage and that the best way to heal was to spend time with friends. Mona had been waiting for this trip, and was glad she could spend more time with Celia, too. It reminded her of the old times in college working on projects, discovering new things, and giggling all the time. Cohen sat next to Mona on the bus, one row back from the front, and she was happy he did. He remarked often on the warm sun and the fresh air in Colorado, as he found it a refreshing change from Chicago. Mona found Cohen to be a refreshing change from her life in Montana.

Mona felt that she was glowing on the reunion trip to Vail. She was so happy and excited to see all of her classmates that she felt healthy, young and alive. The group of travelers quickly retired once they reached the hotel, for they had a busy weekend planned. Cohen, however, was not tired, and, of course, neither was Mona, so they stayed in the lobby. Mona drank hot tea, and Cohen had scotch on the rocks. Mona was so attracted to the way Cohen talked, and while trying to listen to what he was saying, she could only focus on his soft and moist lips. He stared into her, passionately and sexually. They'd occasionally, gently touch and tap each other's bodies when conversing and joking around.

The evening was unintentionally set for romance as the hotel had beautiful flowers on the table, the lights were dim, classical music played in the distance over the speakers and they were completely alone. They had such a connection, and spoke on a level that was surprising, for two adults who had really just met. Mona felt like she was returning to her childhood with the knowledge of a grown woman, and that Cohen was accompanying her. Their memories stretched over geographies and time, and now their feelings had found their way to Vail, where they had been set free to finally explore.

The next two days with the group were full of activities, elaborate meals, and much singing and dancing. Mona sang Egyptian songs, and everyone joined in. Cohen and Mona watched each other closely on the dance floor, and Mona was pleased to see that he was a wonderful dancer. Turns out, Cohen had been ballroom dancing for many years, and he led her around the floor all night. The class reunion was a blast, and Cohen and Mona's time together made them feel reconnected and closer than ever. After the trip, they resolved to stay in touch more frequently.

Their phone conversations, which were random before the reunion, now came twice a week and then, eventually, daily. One day, on the phone, Cohen mentioned that he was planning a trip to California for work, and Mona asked him if he wanted to visit her in Montana on his way. Cohen enthusiastically agreed. Cohen had planned to stay in a hotel and rent a car from the airport, as this fell in accordance to their culture, but Mona insisted that she at the least pick him up at the airport.

Mona could tell he was excited about the visit from the way he talked about it, and Cohen called the night before, on the way to the airport, on the plane, and when he got to Montana. Upon arrival, Cohen's heart was racing nearly out of his chest, and unbeknownst to him, so was Mona's.

They had a wonderful weekend together. Mona gave him the full tour, showing him everything Montana had to offer. He was interested in the architecture of her house because he had built a few houses himself, and he was enthusiastic, as was Mona, about everything they did. In the style of a true gentleman, he bought yellow roses and a beautiful vase for Yasmeen when everyone gathered for a meal. He brought Paulo a bottle of scotch which pleased him as well. The whole family was impressed with his manners and intrigued by his stories about his children, how they were named, and how they were raised. It seemed the entire family, and especially Mona, fell in love with him and his presence.

Cohen had to leave early for his flight on Monday morning, so he insisted on taking a shuttle to the airport. He told Mona that he hoped she would visit him in Chicago whenever she had the opportunity, and Mona agreed to try. Seeing Cohen leave felt strange for Mona, the weekend was too short, and she didn't want it to end yet.

After the visit, they resumed talking to each other whenever they could. Cohen and Mona had been brought closer by their recent life circumstances. They were both single; their children were away from home. They were well-situated with good jobs. They shared common interests and common origins, although they still didn't share the same town.

They took every opportunity to be with each other. Mona was conscious of how happy Cohen's presence made her and how much she looked forward to seeing him again every time he went away. Cohen was sensitive to her needs and had stood by her in the most trying times. He gave Mona enough time and space, but they both knew, as they always had, they were right for each other and were meant to be together.

Then, after four months, she was traveling to DC and stopped for a visit along the way. They were to meet at a coffeehouse in Chicago, and it was a typically windy day. Cohen had arrived early and was waiting for Mona. He watched her get out of the car, walk across the street, come in, and sit before him. As he took in her windswept appearance with admiration, he realized he had to tell her what was on his mind.

"Mona, I think that we've grieved enough for our respective spouses. I think it's time we make the best of our time together and take our relationship a step further."

The abrupt confession startled Mona, but she shrugged it off, saying, "I don't know what you mean, Cohen. We are already so close."

The conversation awkwardly drifted to other topics, and though they hadn't dealt with the matter, neither of them forgot about it. Mona thought about it on the way home, and was ashamed of herself and her fear. She had always been afraid to finally say yes, or let herself be with Cohen, and it cost her greatly. Even though she couldn't admit it to herself, deep down, she still considered Cohen to be different because he was a Jew. She had been working all her life against discrimination of every sort, and now realized that she herself was rejecting him because of her ingrained prejudice. A prejudice that had no regard for the heart, and furthermore, as she was painfully realizing, a prejudice that kept Mona from following her heart.

A Visit to Israel

Mona learned from Cohen that he had accepted a great opportunity, through an important engineering project, and had to travel to Israel. The prospect of visiting his homeland after such a long time was exciting for him. The days before he left were a blur as he made preparations. His perfectionism made him work hard, and the results generally made him a happy man at the end of the day. Finally his day of departure arrived, and Mona had gone to visit for a few days before so she could be there to see him off.

They had a while to sit at the airport lounge and enjoy a quiet lunch, and it somehow brought back memories of their college years in Egypt. They reminisced and wondered if they could ever go back there together and be seen together by their family and old friends. Once lunch was over, Cohen reluctantly left for Israel, and Mona waved good-bye. Both of them parted with a heavy heart but were consoled by the knowledge that they would see each other again as they had always managed to reconnect.

The flight to Israel took about ten hours. Cohen spent most of that time working out the details of his project, and the rest of the time thinking about Mona. Due to the cranky and loud baby in the seat in front of him, Cohen didn't get any sleep. By the time he made it to the Tel Aviv International Airport, he was exhausted and it was morning. The city was bustling with activity, and the locals were rushing to start their work day. Cohen was scheduled to speak to a group about his project later that afternoon, and when he landed at the airport, the hosts took him straight to the conference venue. He gave his presentation, although he was feeling jetlagged, and received a lot of feedback for his work. This new insight motivated some revisions to his original ideas and Cohen pushed beyond his limits and worked, tirelessly, for the rest of the week. He was overexerted, fatigued, and not resting, and his body was feeling the effects. As his return to the United States drew close, things took a turn for the worse.

The weather in Tel Aviv was hot, and mosquitoes carrying the West Nile virus ran rampant that season. In his preoccupation with work, Cohen had forgotten to take his prophylactic immunization against the virus when he left the United States. To make matters worse, he hadn't bothered to spray on mosquito repellent or close his windows at the hotel, which had been advised.

His exhaustion made him, and his immune system, all the more vulnerable. It wasn't long before he came down with a high fever and chills accompanied by overwhelming fatigue. He was all alone, which only made his misery more unbearable. He wished Mona was by his side, he wished he's see her one more time. When he hadn't improved, in the next couple of days, he decided to return to the States to see his doctor back home; even though the risk of travel in his condition was considered foolish.

All the while, Mona was eagerly waiting to hear from Cohen as she expected his return. She wondered how things had worked out for him at the conference. She was blissfully unaware of how seriously ill he was when she received a call from him the day he left Israel, two days sooner than planned. She was now restless and hopelessly worried for him and his journey home. The travel would only make him weaker and she didn't want him to take the chance in his condition. She got to the airport about two hours before his arrival time, as she just couldn't wait any longer at her hotel with her restlessness and worry.

At last, he arrived in Chicago and as she saw him get off the tarmac, the sight of him made her heart ache. He looked haggard, his eyes sunken and his complexion deathly pale. An airline employee wheeled him out on a wheelchair, which made him look older and sicker than he probably was. In spite of his sickness, the sight of Mona brought a smile to his face, but smiling took considerable effort. Cohen was rushed to the hospital directly from the airport with a fever of one hundred and four.

As the doctors had warned, the travel had taken a toll on his health. His vital signs were dangerously low, and even the doctors seemed worried. He slipped in and out of consciousness. His doctors were losing hope and called for his family and close friends to come visit and be close by. Throughout this ordeal, Mona never left his side, even though he was in the intensive care unit, where only family members were given admission. Cohen called out for her in the few moments when he regained consciousness, and she was there every time.

The fifth day of his stay in the ICU was particularly bleak for Cohen. He remained unconscious for most of the day, and when he finally regained consciousness, he had a feeling of impending doom. He saw the dejected look on the doctors' faces and felt the end was near. He wanted to spend each and every waking moment he had left with Mona. He requested that she get a Quran and Torah as quickly as possible. Mona was happy to be of service in any way, but watching him lie lifelessly in bed was taking its toll on her. Mona had to go to the hospital chapel for the books and by the time she got back to his side, the nurses had propped him up and given him a copy of the Bible which he was perusing.

He handed Mona the Bible so she could continue for him as he had lost even more strength in her short trip to the chapel. He looked at her and, in a calm voice, asked her to read out a few passages he had marked so that he could cross over to the next world in peace, hearing the word of God from the Bible had soothed him, as the Torah had done all his life. Mona opened the Bible and read the verses as instructed in a soft voice:

"The Bible reads, in Proverbs 13 'Love is patient, love is kind. It does not envy, it does not boast, it is not proud. It is not rude, it is not self-seeking, it is not easily angered, it keeps no record of wrongs. Love does not delight in evil but rejoices with the truth. It always protects, always trusts, always hopes, always perseveres. Love never fails . . . And now these three remain: faith, hope, and love. But the greatest of these is love.'"

As Mona continued to read aloud, now from the Torah, she found the passage he had selected and she repeated to Cohen, "The Torah reads, in Leviticus 18:18, 'Do not take revenge and do not bear a grudge. Love your neighbor as yourself. I am God.'"

This time she was reading from the Koran, and Mona found the particular passage that Cohen lastly had selected. She asked Cohen if he was still listening and as he nodded she read, "The Koran reads, Al-Rum 30:21, '"And of His signs is that He created mates for you from yourselves that you might find peace of mind in them, and He put between you love and compassion . . ."'"

As Mona read the verses, she realized that all the passages Cohen had selected revealed that all life and all religions were based on love, peace, and forgiveness. All three religions shared a common foundation. She was struck by his knowledge of other religions, as it signaled how exceptionally open-minded he was, and his willingness to think outside of his comfort zone. Mona envied that about Cohen as she realized he had thought about this concept for years, maybe their whole lives. She regretted her own narrow-mindedness and rigid adherence to her own religion without pausing to understand the beliefs and teachings of other religions. She also regretted that she had created a wall of prejudice around Cohen and had denied herself the experience of a sincere relationship with him based on true love.

The potential loss of Cohen created havoc in Mona's mind. She had much remorse for wasting opportunities to spend time with him in the past. She remembered the day, years ago in Egypt, when he had asked her out for the very first time. Mona thought of the time she spent with Cohen in childhood, the time he had supported her through her grief, and the time he had professed his love for her as it all flashed before her eyes. How she wished she could turn back time. At that very moment, she knew she couldn't hide from the truth anymore. With tears in her eyes, Mona finally uttered the words, "I love you, Cohen!" Barely able to lift his head towards Mona, Cohen softly said, "I have longed all my life to hear you say those words out loud to me Mona, thank you my love."

Thinking again of all the words she had read in the holy books, Mona secretly made a pledge to herself. She prayed that if God were to keep Cohen alive, she would never deny her love or keep herself away from him anymore. She would make a conscious effort to overcome her meaningless prejudice and would display her feelings for Cohen openly. She would no longer try to fool herself into believing that she did not love Cohen.

Please, God, keep him alive. Give me one more chance, Mona fervently prayed as she waited anxiously at the hospital chapel for Cohen to recover. Cohen recognized the genuine expression of Mona's feelings for him and felt that if he were to die that very day, he wouldn't mind. But he never gave up hope and fought hard for his life. Miraculously, the moment of dread passed as quickly as it had come. In the next few days, his health improved, and even the doctors were amazed by his recovery. Cohen was well again!

It seemed as if in no time, Cohen had fully recovered from his illness. He believed he had been given a second life and another chance. Mona let all her barriers down and was fully committed to Cohen even though they were still living in different cities. They made the most of their times together.

Cohen had heard from Celia that she was planning another class reunion, this time in Egypt, and he suggested to Mona that they travel together to the reunion and spend a few extra days alone in Cairo, Alexandria, and Sinai. Then they could vacation on the beach and swim in the Mediterranean Sea and enjoy their native land together as a couple.

"Absolutely!" Mona said ecstatically. She was really looking forward to reconnecting with fellow Egyptians at the reunion, and she also looked forward to her time alone with Cohen after. The reunion was memorable and they both enjoyed catching up with their old friends and their country's flair for good parties. The weekend was quick and they were on a train to Alexandria before they knew it.

It was a warm April day, nearly ninety degrees, and the humidity of the air was evident in the moist skin of the locals. Mona and Cohen swam in circles around each other and then stood simultaneously in the waist-deep water. Because Mona wasn't wearing shoes, her feet slid in the sand, and as she was about to fall, Cohen quickly caught her in his strong arms. They had no reason to resist. The time had come. Their first kiss was on the beach in Alexandria, and they kissed until sunset. Mona couldn't imagine being happier as she was waist deep in the Mediterranean Sea in the arms of the man she loved.

That night in the hotel, where Mona and Cohen were staying, they met in the lobby, and Cohen told her he had something to say. Mona's heart began to beat faster. Cohen took her hands in his and said, "I've waited so long for this moment. I have loved you since I first knew what love was. Mona, will you marry me?"

Mona could only say, "Yes, Cohen, yes! I will!"

The rest of their stay in Alexandria was magnificent and felt as if they had skipped right to the honeymoon. They soon returned to the United States and started planning a quiet wedding ceremony to mark their new life together and honor their love. Their children were excited for them, and so were Isis and Celia who were the only friends that they had told. Cohen and Mona put off thinking about their extended families back home in Egypt and Israel for now; they figured they could deal with them later. Nothing could come between Mona and Cohen now, love had victoriously found its way back to them and they would never let it go again.

Epilogue

The End. "The End?" Jackie questions. Jackie, my young passenger, seems dissatisfied. "Love prevails Jackie," I begin to say, "Racism, ethnicity, career and money mean nothing. It is love that is important, and it comes in every shape and size." I merge off the highway into Johnson, and easily find the shelter. I park in the lot and wait to assure Jackie will be okay from here. Jackie begins to reveal her discontent, "Where is Mona now? Did she and Cohen get married? Did they live happily ever after? Did their parents accept their love for each other?" I shake my head, explaining that I still had a twenty-mile drive to the cemetery, and

I reach for the bouquet of flowers which I had placed in the back seat. "What kind of flowers are those?" Jackie asks, "I meant to ask you earlier, but was so captivated with the story that I forgot." At that exact moment, my telephone rings which I expected as I had only a couple of hours to myself and, by now, had well exceeded them. "Hello," I say as I answer the call, "Hang on a minute, I'll be right back with you." I place my phone down on the car's dashboard, grab a flower out of the bouquet and hand it to Jackie as I say, "This flower is for you, may it remind you that love always wins if you are true to your heart, Jackie. I don't know what the flower is called, but it looks almost identical to the sesen—the Egyptian lotus."

Dr. Omnia El-Hakim

Dr. Omnia El-Hakim has an established record of leadership in community service and academia.

Since January 2009, Dr. El-Hakim accepted an IPA (Intergovernmental Personnel Act) assignment at the National Science Foundation, becoming Director for Diversity and Outreach in the Directorate of Engineering. She has responsibility for establishing sustainable diversity programs that bridge all learning communities from K-12 to post-graduate levels. Dr. El-Hakim is responsible for envisioning ways to accomplish NSF's strategic goals as they relate to broadening participation in the engineering community that enhances equity and diversity. One of Dr. El-Hakim's visions, besides increasing the number of women and underrepresented groups in engineering disciplines, is to reach out to international communities to provide collaborative opportunities that will benefit students and faculty gaining international experiences.

Before NSF, she joined Colorado State University, Fort Collins, CO, in 1984 while holding a joint appointment as Professor of Civil Engineering at Fort Lewis College in, Durango, CO where she also served as Department Chair of Physics and Engineering from 1996-1999. In addition, Dr. El-Hakim served as Assistant Dean for Diversity of the College of Engineering at Colorado State University from 2003-2006. Diversity is El-Hakim's passion; she created and led a Colorado Consortium of 14 universities, community and four-year colleges, and tribal Nations as Principal Investigator and Director of the Colorado Alliance for Minority Participation (CO-AMP), as well as several other diversity programs for 20 years. She developed diversity programs to assist underrepresented minority students from K-12 to graduate schools. Dr. El-Hakim obtained her doctoral degree in Civil Engineering from Colorado State University (1984) after completing her undergraduate studies and receiving a Masters Degree in Civil Engineering from Cairo University in Egypt (1977).

Dr. El-Hakim has tremendous experience in conducting international water resources activities and management projects. In this capacity, she directed efforts to collaborate activities between the country of Egypt and the United States of America ((1980-1995) in order to organize and train engineers and scientists in the area of water resources' management in both the Arabic and English languages. The success of the activities resulted in a production of more than 200 individuals (where there were approximately 30-35% women in science and engineering) who received doctoral degrees and are now holding leadership positions in the country of Egypt.

Dr. El-Hakim is a steadfast advocate for women, underrepresented minorities and persons with disabilities across the nation. Her goal is to collaborate with existing programs in the NSF directorates and other federal agencies, as well as national professional societies, to expand and create new outreach opportunities of excellence. At NSF, Dr. El-hakim was the program director of the NSF BRIGE program (Broadening Participation Research Initiation Grants in Engineering) and GRDS (Graduate Research Diversity Supplements). Indicative of her passion of assisting women navigating STEM (Science, Technology, Engineering and Mathematics) careers in academia, Dr.

El-Hakim was selected by the NSF Director as one of the core members to create the Career Life Balance initiative (2011/12). She received the NSF Director's Equal Opportunity Achievement Award in 2010 as well as the NSF Director's Award for Collaborative Integration in 2012.